ALSO BY ANNE TYLER

If Morning Ever Comes
The Tin Can Tree
A Slipping-Down Life
The Clock Winder
Celestial Navigation
Searching for Caleb
Earthly Possessions
Morgan's Passing
Dinner at the Homesick Restaurant
The Accidental Tourist
Breathing Lessons
Saint Maybe
Ladder of Years
A Patchwork Planet
Back When We Were Grownups
The Amateur Marriage
Digging to America
Noah's Compass
The Beginner's Goodbye
A Spool of Blue Thread
Vinegar Girl
Clock Dance
Redhead by the Side of the Road
French Braid

THREE DAYS
IN JUNE

THREE DAYS
IN JUNE

Anne Tyler

ALFRED A. KNOPF
NEW YORK 2025

THIS IS A BORZOI BOOK
PUBLISHED BY ALFRED A. KNOPF

Copyright © 2025 by Anne Tyler

Penguin Random House values and supports copyright. Copyright fuels creativity, encourages diverse voices, promotes free speech and creates a vibrant culture. Thank you for buying an authorized edition of this book and for complying with copyright laws by not reproducing, scanning, or distributing any part of it in any form without permission. You are supporting writers and allowing Penguin Random House to continue to publish books for every reader. Please note that no part of this book may be used or reproduced in any manner for the purpose of training artificial intelligence technologies or systems.

All rights reserved. Published in the United States by Alfred A. Knopf, a division of Penguin Random House LLC, New York.

www.aaknopf.com

Knopf, Borzoi Books, and the colophon are registered trademarks of Penguin Random House LLC.

LIBRARY OF CONGRESS CATALOGING-IN-PUBLICATION DATA
Names: Tyler, Anne, author.
Title: Three days in June / Anne Tyler.
Description: First Edition. | New York : Alfred A. Knopf, 2025.
Identifiers: LCCN 2024008835 (print) | LCCN 2024008836 (ebook) | ISBN 9780593803486 (hardcover) | ISBN 9780593689325 (trade paperback) | ISBN 9780593803493 (eBook) | ISBN 9781524712808 (open market)
Subjects: LCGFT: Novels.
Classification: LCC PS3570.Y45 T497 2025 (print) | LCC PS3570.Y45 (ebook) | DDC 813/.6—dc23/eng/20240226
LC record available at https://lccn.loc.gov/2024008835
LC ebook record available at https://lccn.loc.gov/2024008836

Jacket paintings: (house) David Arsenault. All Rights Reserved 2024 / Bridgeman Images; (cat) Phil Pascuzzo
Jacket design by Kelly Blair

Manufactured in the United States of America
Published February 11, 2025
Second Printing, February 2025

one

DAY OF BEAUTY

People don't tap their watches anymore; have you noticed? Standard wristwatches, I'm talking about. Remember how people used to tap them?

My father, for instance. His watch was a Timex with a face as big as a fifty-cent piece, and whenever my mother kept him waiting he would frown down at it and give it a tap. Implying, I suppose now, "Can this possibly be correct? Could it really be this late?" But when I was a little girl, I imagined he was trying to make time move faster—to bring my mother before us instantly, already wearing her coat, like someone in a speeded-up movie.

What reminded me of this recently was that Marilee Burton, the headmistress at the school where I worked, called me into her office one Friday morning as I was walking past. "Come chat for a moment, why don't you?" she said. This was not a regular occurrence. (We were on more or less formal terms.) She waved toward the Windsor chair facing her desk, but I stayed in the doorway and cocked my head at her.

"I thought I should let you know," she said, "I won't be coming in on Monday. I have to have a cardioversion."

"A what?" I asked.

"A procedure for my heart. It's been beating wrong."

"Oh," I said. I couldn't pretend to be surprised. She was one of those ladylike women who wear heels on all occasions, the perfect candidate for heart issues. "Well, I'm sorry to hear that," I told her.

"They're giving it an electrical jolt that will stop it and then start it again."

"Huh," I said. "Like tapping a watch."

"Pardon?"

"Is it dangerous?" I asked.

"No, no," she said. "I've had it done once before, in fact. But that was over spring break, so I didn't see the need to announce it."

"Okay," I said. "And how long will you be out of the office?"

"I'll be back on Tuesday, good as new. No need to alter your routine in the slightest. *However*," she said, and then she sat straighter behind her desk; she cleared her throat; she briskly aligned a stack of papers that didn't need aligning. "However, it brings me to a subject I've been meaning to discuss with you."

I stood a bit straighter myself. I am very alert to people's tones of voice.

"I'll be sixty-six years old on my next birthday," she said, "and Ralph just turned sixty-eight. He's starting to talk about traveling a bit, and seeing more of the grandchildren."

"Really."

"So I'm thinking of handing in my resignation before the new school year begins."

The new school year would begin in September. We were already in late June.

I said, "So . . . does this mean I'll take over as headmistress?"

It was a perfectly logical question, right? *Somebody* had to do it. And I was next in line, for sure. I'd been Marilee's assistant for the past eleven years. But Marilee let a small silence develop, as if I'd presumed in some way. Then she said, "Well, that's what I wanted to chat about."

She selected the top sheet on her stack of papers, and she turned it around to face me and slid it across her desk. I stepped forward, grudgingly. I squinted at it. A typewritten page with a newspaper clipping stapled to one corner—a black-and-white photo of a serious young woman with energetically curly dark hair. "Nashville Educator's Study on Learning Differences Wins McLellan Prize," the headline read.

I said, "Nashville?" (We lived in Baltimore.) And I had no idea what the McLellan Prize was.

"I brought her name to the board's attention when I first began to think of retiring," Marilee said. "Dorothy Edge; maybe you've heard of her. I'd read her book, you see, and I'd found it very impressive."

"You brought her to the board's attention," I repeated.

"After all, Gail," she said. "You're sixty-one years old, am I right? You won't be working much longer yourself."

"I'm sixty-one years old!" I said. "Nowhere near retirement age!"

"It's not only a matter of age," she told me. She was looking at me with her chin raised, the way people do when they know they're in the wrong. "Face it: this job is a matter of people skills. *You* know that! And surely you'll be the first to admit that social interactions have never been your strong point."

"What are you talking about?" I asked her. "What possible interactions could you be referring to?"

"I mean, of course you have many other skills," Marilee

said. "You're much more organized than I am. You're a much better public speaker. But look at just now, for instance. I tell you I have a heart condition and you just say, 'Oh,' and pass right on to the question of taking over my job."

"I said, 'Oh,'" I reminded her. "I said, 'I'm sorry to hear that.'" (Another of my strengths is that I have a very good audial memory, including for my own words.) "What more did you require of me?"

"I 'required' nothing at all," she said, and now her chin was practically pointed at the ceiling. "All I'm saying is, to head a private girls' school you need tact. You need diplomacy. You need to avoid saying things like 'Good God, Mrs. Morris, surely you realize your daughter doesn't have the slightest chance of getting into Princeton.'"

"Katy Morris couldn't get into a decent *trade* school," I said.

"That's not the point," Marilee said.

"So?" I said. "Just because I refuse to sweet-talk all your rich-guy parents I'm doomed to stay on forever as assistant headmistress?"

"Or," Marilee said, and now she lowered her chin and gazed at me directly across the expanse of her desk. "Perhaps *not* stay on."

"Excuse me?"

"Think of some new occupation, perhaps," she suggested. "Strike out in a whole new direction. Do something you've always dreamed of doing; what do you say?"

I wondered what on earth she imagined that might be. I am not the kind of woman who dreams of doing things.

"Dottie, I mean Dr. Edge, has expressed a wish that we bring in the assistant she's been working with in Nashville,"

Marilee said. "Apparently the two of them have formed quite an effective team together."

Dottie.

All this time, I'd been clasping my purse with both hands in front of me. (Marilee had caught me on my way to my office, at the very start of the day.) Now I felt like some sort of beggar, like someone lacing her fingers together and pleading for a favor, and I dropped my purse to my left side. "Well," I said, "I hope they'll both be very happy here. Good-bye, Marilee."

"Gail?"

I spun on my heel and walked out.

"Gail, *please* don't be like this!"

I walked back down the hall to the foyer, past the trophy case, and out the front door to the street.

Didn't even stop to collect the pen-and-pencil set on my desk, or the photo of my daughter in her cap and gown, or the cardigan I kept hanging in the closet. Someone could send it all to me later, I thought. Or throw it out; what did I care?

In the parking lot there were only three cars—Marilee's and mine and the custodian's. The sky overhead was gray and looming—rain had been forecast for later—and the two workmen setting traffic cones on the nearby sidewalk wore bright orange slickers. I got into my Corolla and started the engine and took off immediately, not even pausing to roll down my window, although the interior felt like an oven already. I couldn't bear to be observed, was why. I felt embarrassed; I felt conspicuous.

Although it wasn't as if this were *my* fault!

I lived in a neighborhood so close to the school that sometimes I walked to work, but I had driven that morning because

I'd been planning to stop by the cleaner's afterward and pick up the dress I'd be wearing that evening. It was the evening of my daughter's wedding rehearsal, with dinner to follow. But now I couldn't imagine attending, even. I pictured sitting in the half-empty church while the rest of the wedding party pointed at me and whispered. "Poor, poor Gail," they would whisper. "Have you heard?"

She was let go, at age sixty-one.

Lacks people skills.

Wasn't even consulted about her daughter's Day of Beauty today at Darleen's Spa and Massage. The groom's mother set that up entirely on her own. (What could *Gail* have contributed? she must have thought. Such a ... right-angled person, such a pale-faced, straight-haired person who doesn't care in the least about looks!)

But they could at least have discussed it with me. I was the mother of the bride.

Never mind that I hadn't known there was even such a thing as a Day of Beauty.

I didn't stop by the cleaner's. I drove directly home. I parked at the curb and climbed the steps to the porch, unlocked the door, and walked into the living room and sank into the first chair I came to, facing the front window. A gauzy white curtain misted the view, so no one could look in and see me. Grandpa Simmons's mantel clock ticked on the bookcase. I didn't possess an actual mantel. This was a very small, very unassuming house, two-bedroom, built sometime in the sixties. TV set so old that it stuck out in back a good foot and a half. Crocheted afghan draped over one couch arm to hide where the upholstery had worn down to bare threads. I did own the house outright, though. I bought it with the money my father left me. I could have taken over my parents' house, since my mother moved to a high-rise immediately after his death, but by that time my marriage was already on rocky ground and I knew that what I needed was a place I could maintain on my own without needing to count on Max. I don't mean that Max was a deadbeat, or anything like that; it was just that he had a tendency to choose low-paying jobs. To this day, he lived hand to mouth—taught at a school for at-risk teenagers over on the Eastern Shore. Rented a one-room apartment above somebody's garage.

No one had ever told me before that I lacked people skills. Not in so many words, at least. It was true that my one-time mother-in-law had given me a copy of *Manners for the Mystified*, but that was just... pro forma, right? All brides could use an etiquette book! She didn't mean anything by it.

I wrote her a thank-you note for that book just to prove that my manners were fine, and then Max suggested that maybe we could invite his parents to dinner and I could go to extremes on the etiquette—offer finger bowls after the soup or something. He was joking, of course. I don't think we ever did have his parents to dinner.

Did Marilee imagine that I was independently wealthy? I couldn't *afford* to quit work!

The clock gathered itself together with a whirring of gears and struck a series of blurry notes. Nine o'clock, I was thinking; but no, it turned out to be ten. I'd been sitting there in a sort of stupor, evidently. I stood up and hung my purse in the closet, but then outside the window I saw some movement on the other side of the curtain, some dark and ponderous shape laboring up my front walk. I tweaked the curtain aside a half inch. Max, for God's sake. Max with a duffel bag slung over one shoulder, and a bulky square suitcase dangling from his left hand.

I went to the front door and opened it and looked out at him through the screen. "What on earth?" I asked him.

"You're home!" he said.

"Yes..."

"Debbie is at something called a Day of Beauty."

"Right," I said.

"But she knew ahead I was coming. I told her I was coming. I get there and no one's home. I call her cell phone and she says she didn't expect me so early."

"Why *did* you come so early?" I asked him.

"I wanted to beat the rush. You know what Fridays are like on the Bay Bridge."

All the more reason not to live on the other side of it, I could have pointed out. I opened the screen door for him and reached for his suitcase, but it wasn't a suitcase; it was some kind of animal carrier. Square patch of wire grid on the end and something watchful and alert staring out from behind it gleaming-eyed. Max moved the carrier away from me a bit and said, "I've got it."

"What is it?"

"It's a cat."

"A cat!"

"Could I come in, do you think?"

I retreated and he lumbered in, out of breath, shaking the floorboards. Max was nowhere near fat, but he was *weighty*, broad shouldered; he always gave the impression of taking up more than his share of room, although he was not much taller than I was. In the years since we'd divorced he had grown the kind of beard that you're not quite sure is deliberate; maybe he'd merely forgotten to shave for a while. A short gray frizzle with a frizzle of gray hair to match, and he seemed to have given up on his clothes; generally he wore stretched-out knit tops and baggy khakis. I hoped he'd brought a suit for the wedding. You never could be sure.

"Couldn't you have just left your cat at home with food and water?" I asked, following him through the living room. "I mean, it's already bad enough that you're staying with Debbie yourself. In the middle of her wedding preparations, for God's sake!"

"She said it would be fine if I stayed," Max told me. "She said it wasn't a problem."

"Okay, but then to add a cat to the mix . . . Cats do very well on their own. They almost prefer it, in fact."

"Not this one," he said. He set the carrier on my kitchen counter. "This one is too new."

"It's a kitten?"

"No, no, it's old."

"You just said—"

"It's an elderly female cat who belonged to a very old woman, and now the woman has up and died and the cat is in mourning," he told me.

There was a lot I could have asked about this, but it didn't seem worth the effort. I leaned closer to peer at the cat. "Does Debbie know you're bringing it?" I asked him.

"Now she does."

I waited.

"It's complicated," he said. He blotted his face on his shoulder. "I phoned her; I said, 'Where *are* you?' She says she's at a Day of Beauty. 'Did you leave a key out someplace?' I asked her, and she says no, but she'll be home in a few hours. 'A few hours!' I say. 'I can't wait a few hours! I've got a cat here!' She says, 'A what?' Then she hits the roof. Tells me I can in no way bring a cat to her house, because Kenneth is allergic."

"He is?" I said.

"*Deathly* allergic, is how she put it."

"But . . . Kenneth doesn't live there," I said.

"Don't kid yourself," Max told me. "You know he stays over a lot, and besides, he does plan to live there after the wedding."

"Well, sure, *after* the wedding."

"'Deathly' allergic, Gail. As in, if he walks into a house where a cat has left a smidgen of dander behind, even if the cat is long gone he'll need a respirator."

"A respirator!"

"Or whatever you call those things that asthmatics have to carry around with them."

"You mean an atomizer," I said.

"No, not an atomizer; a what's-it. A vaporizer, maybe?"

I thought it over.

"At any rate, that's what Debbie claimed. She claimed that even if he's just standing next to her and she has cat dander on her sweater, he will start choking up and he'll need a . . ."

We both stood there, considering.

The cat said, "Hmm?"

We looked over at the carrier.

"Anyhow," Max said, and he unfastened the two latches and lifted the lid. Instead of stepping out, the cat hunched lower and stared up at me. A gray-and-black tabby with a chunky face. "So I couldn't think where to go except here," Max said. "I knew where you hide *your* key. It didn't occur to me that you would be home on a weekday."

"Yes, well . . . ," I said. And then I told the cat, "Hey there." She squared her eyes at me.

"What's her name?" I asked Max.

"I don't know."

"What? How could you not know?"

"I'm just the fosterer," he told me. "I volunteer at this shelter where they need people to foster animals until they can be adopted. Ordinarily it's kittens, batches of feral kittens that need domesticating first, but this one's a senior citizen. I'm thinking of naming her 'Pearl,' at least for as long as I have her around."

"Pearl!"

"On account of her color."

"You can't name a cat 'Pearl.'"

"Why not?"

"Cats are so bad at language," I told him. "They're not the least bit like dogs. Cats just get your general tone, and 'Pearl' has a tone like a growl."

"It does?"

"So does 'Ruby.' So does 'Rhinestone.'"

"Aha!" Max said. "See there? Everything turns out for the best."

"It does?" I said. "What are you talking about?"

"You can advise me on cat lore," he said. "Plus you might even decide to adopt her; who knows?"

"Max," I said, "sometimes I wonder if you understand the least little thing about me."

"But you love cats! You used to have that homely little calico cat. And this one's accustomed to older women."

"Thanks," I said.

" 'Older,' I said. Not 'old.' "

"I do not want a cat in any way, shape, or form," I told him.

"What do you think of 'Mary?' " he asked. "Or 'Carol.' How about that?"

"Forget it, Max," I said. Then I added, "And you want to steer away from the *r* sound. An *r* is a growl, straight out."

"Oh, right. Yes. Thank you." He paused. "How about 'Lucy'?" he said.

"Forget it, I told you."

He sighed.

"Maybe you could drop her off at a shelter here in Baltimore," I said. "I mean, surely they wouldn't refuse her."

"We're not allowed to just dump our charges any-old-where," he told me. "No, I'd better keep her here at your house, and then take her back to Cornboro if you really don't want her."

"I most emphatically do not want her," I said. Then, "Nor do I want a houseguest."

"Yes, but, see, there's dander all over my clothes now. I can't possibly go back to Debbie's, even without the cat."

"In fact, I wonder if you should come to the wedding, even," I said. "Just think if Kenneth starts choking during the vows."

This was pure mischief, on my part. I seriously doubted that Kenneth would choke; he'd always struck me as a sturdy type of guy.

But Max looked stricken. He said, "Not attend my own daughter's wedding?"

"Well, you could maybe wear a raincoat," I said. "Or one of those hazmat suits."

The kitchen phone rang. We both glanced over at it. It rang again, and then a third time. "Aren't you going to get that?" Max asked me.

But I was thinking it might be Marilee, and sure enough, after my outgoing message Marilee came on and asked, "Gail? Are you there?"

This was why I still had an actual, physical answering machine: there were too many people I might not feel like talking to.

"Because we really need to discuss this," Marilee said. "Could you pick up, please?"

Max wrinkled his forehead at me.

"Ignore that," I told him.

"What's going on?"

"Nothing's going on."

"Okay..."

The answering machine clicked off, and I turned back to the cat. I briefly closed my eyes at her. Cats take that as reassurance; to them it's like a smile. Then I looked off in another direction. I heard a rustle, and when I slid a glance sideways I saw her unfolding herself from the carrier by degrees and stepping gingerly onto the counter. "A little weight problem," I murmured.

As if to demonstrate, she landed on the floor with a noticeable thud.

"I think it's from stress," Max said. "Apparently she'd been alone for some time before anyone realized her owner had died."

I made a sympathetic *tsk*ing sound.

"What's up with Marilee?" Max asked. He'd never been very good at minding his own business.

I said, "Nothing's up with Marilee."

The cat was heading into the living room now, so I made a big show of following her. She paused to sniff at the fringe on the rug and then padded over to an armchair and sprang into it, more nimbly than you might expect.

"What does she want to discuss?" Max asked, trailing after me.

I gave up. I said, "She's retiring in the fall and she wants the board to hire this other person in her place, this Nashville person. And the Nashville person is asking to bring in her own assistant. So I'm thinking I should just quit before they fire me."

"Excellent," Max said.

I turned to look at him.

"Your great talent is for teaching; you know that," Max said. "Dealing with all the kids who are scared to death of math."

"You're forgetting that teachers make no money, though," I told him. "Why else did I put in all that hell time getting my master's degree?"

"So? Now that Debbie's finished law school, you can go back to doing what you're good at."

"It's not that simple," I told him.

Still, it was nice of him to say that I was good at something.

But then he changed the subject. "Guess I might as well bring in the cat supplies," he said. And he went on outside, leaving the front door open behind him even though the air conditioning was on.

I turned back to the cat. She was a bread-loaf shape in the

armchair now with her front paws folded beneath her, and when she saw me looking at her she shut her eyes lazily and then opened them again.

Max came back with a sack of cat kibble stashed in a brown plastic tub, a larger sack of kitty litter swinging from his free hand. "Where do you think for the litter box? Kitchen?" he asked me.

"No, not the kitchen! Good grief! The powder room, I guess."

He headed toward the powder room. Of course the front door was still open. I went over and slammed it shut.

When he returned he had collected his duffel bag from the kitchen, and he started up the stairs with it. "Sheets in the bathroom closet?" he called back to me.

"You won't need sheets; the bed's already made up," I said.

"Ha! It's a good thing my mother's not alive," he said. "You remember how she couldn't countenance a guest bed with unfresh bedding."

"Oh, she couldn't, could she?" I asked in a mocking tone. "She couldn't 'countenance' it, could she?" I was climbing after him; I had just recalled that the bed was covered with old photographs that I'd been going through for a display at Debbie's reception. "*Manners for the Mystified*," I said.

"Huh?"

I swept into the guest room ahead of him and started gathering the photos, completely messing up all the sorting I'd been doing. "Why, look at that!" Max said in a marveling tone. "Us at Bethany Beach."

He had picked up a wallet-size photo that was lying on one pillow, all crinkly-edged like olden times. Max and I very young and unformed, and Debbie as cute as a button in one of those bathing suits with a ballerina skirt. I wasn't going to use that one; Kenneth's mother had specified that the photos should be four-by-sixes. Still, Debbie looked so darling! She had those dusty pale freckles she always got in the summer, that magically faded away every year by Thanksgiving. I took the picture from Max and stared down at it. "You should go back to wearing your hair long," Max told me.

"Mutton dressed as lamb," I said.

"What?"

I added the photo to my stack of photos and turned to leave the room with them. Then I glanced back at Max. I said, "*You* don't think I lack people skills, do you?"

"Hmm?" he said.

"Marilee feels I lack people skills."

"Is that a fact," he said.

But I could tell he wasn't paying full attention. He had set his duffel bag on the bed and started unzipping it.

"I mean, I know I'm not Ms. Social Butterfly," I told him, "but in a lot of ways, I hold that school together! Look at during Covid times: I was the only one who went in to work every day. Dealt with the mail and the service people and even let this one pushy father come in for a tour. With all the windows open, of course."

"Right," Max said. He drew a cylinder of wrinkled khaki from his duffel and unrolled it—a sports coat. He held it up to examine it.

"It takes real restraint to talk face-to-face with a man who wears his mask below his nose," I said.

Max said, "Here's a thought. You know how in the area where I live, there are all these senior citizens. These people who've settled on the Eastern Shore after they retired. So what

I've always thought is, someone should open a grocery store called 'The Singles Bar.' Get it?"

I said, "The . . . ?"

"Everything would be available in single-size portions. One carrot, not a whole bag. Two doughnuts, not a dozen. Six spears of asparagus."

I said, "Um . . ."

"Think about it," he urged me.

"Think about it in what way?" I asked.

"Think about opening a grocery store on the Eastern Shore."

I stared at him. "You *do* feel I lack people skills," I told him.

"No, I just meant—"

"First you say I'm so good at curing math anxiety, but then you tell me to get a job selling asparagus! Is that what you really think of me?"

"No, see," he said, "this is where you always go wrong. You just . . . take something I say and run with it, just totally misinterpret it. There's no reasoning with you!"

"Have it your way," I said. Then I said, "Well, I'm off to the cleaner's. Bye."

"What—now?"

"Now," I said.

I left the room. I went downstairs and collected my purse and went out to my car.

Wouldn't you know he had parked so close behind me that I had to perform about six maneuvers before I could take off.

I'd been using the same dry cleaner for years—a little place on Bachelor Street with one small, cross-looking man behind the counter. But he never gave a sign that he'd laid eyes on me before, so this morning I passed him my receipt without a word and he accepted it silently and went to take a dress from the rack. This was my official Parents' Night shirtwaist, light gray. For the wedding itself I planned to wear my best outfit, a silk-like dress in a darker gray. (I don't do well with colors.) Debbie had offered to help me shop for a mother-of-the-bride dress, but I didn't see the point in paying a lot of money for something I'd wear only once.

I hung the shirtwaist from a hook in my car, and I was just about to settle behind the wheel when I happened to glance toward the place I'd parked in front of: Sheila's Hair Salon. I hesitated. Then I shut the driver's-side door again.

It was a *tiny* salon. One chair. No wonder I'd never noticed it before. And not a person to be seen. "Hello?" I called.

Footsteps approached from the rear of the shop, and out came a youngish woman with very brightly dyed pink hair that hung to her shoulder on one side but was slashed off above her ear on the other side. "Oh," I said. Then I said, "I don't actually have an appointment..." I was backing toward the door as I spoke. "Maybe I'll phone later and—"

"That's okay; it so happens I'm free right now," the woman said. "What did you want done?"

"Um, some kind of ... um, fluffing? For my daughter's wedding? But I really—"

"I can do that!" she said. "When's she getting married?"

"Tomorrow. Plus today there's a rehearsal dinner."

"Oh, cool! Have a seat," the woman said.

She waved toward the chair, and I got into it. It had been years since I'd been to a beauty parlor, but I seemed to remember that first there'd been a sort of settling-in process where they took my purse and stashed it someplace close at hand. Not here, though. I sat erect with my purse standing upright on my knees, and I felt more like an applicant than a customer. Meanwhile, the woman was circling me. She picked up one strand of my hair and then let it drop, as if it hadn't quite passed inspection. "What do you think: a little trim?" she asked me.

"No!" I said. Not only had Max implied that my hair was too short as it was (jaw level, more or less), but also I worried that this woman might chop it off asymmetrically. "Just something to show I tried," I told her. "I don't want people to think I didn't care enough."

"Right," she said. She took a folded wrap from one of the shelves and shook it out and draped it over me, purse and all. "How would you feel about a bit of a tint?" she asked me.

"No, thanks."

I have that kind of blond hair that just sort of gradually fades, and I could only imagine how garish I'd look with anything else. "If you could pouf it out a bit, is all," I said. "Make it not so much hanging down."

She said, "Sure." But she sounded disappointed.

The reason I stay away from beauty parlors is, I never know what to talk about there. I mean, those places are real gabfests! The last time I went, I was in high school—I did say it had been years, right?—and I remember I was in the middle of getting a sort of beehive arrangement for junior prom when I heard the customer next to me say, "Well, I finally got to lay eyes on the Other Woman."

The beautician said, "Ooh!" and stopped with her scissors in midair to give the customer a goggle-eyed stare. "How did *that* happen?" she asked.

"They were coming out of Morgan Millard together. They

were laughing away, all cooey-dovey—didn't even notice I was standing there, thank God."

"Did she look anything like you?" the beautician asked. "You know how I always say the husband tends to go for the same type of woman all over again."

"Not a bit like me. Kind of mousy, in fact. Mousy brown pageboy. I am a *lot* more attractive, if it doesn't sound stuck-up to say so."

"Well, there you are," the beautician said. "What can I tell you."

What could *I* tell *my* beautician to compare with that? was my question. I was a skinny seventeen-year-old at the time, with a full set of braces. Since I'd entered the shop my entire conversation had consisted of "Gail Simmons? Four o'clock?" after which I had handed over a magazine photo of the style I wanted. Period.

So after that visit, I just cut my own hair. It's not that difficult, really; just a matter of remembering that you need to cut the back a little shorter than you would suppose in order to make up for how you've drawn it forward.

It seemed nothing much had changed since then. Sixty-one years old now, going on sixty-two, and I sat through a shampoo, a combing, and a ridiculous amount of blow-drying in total silence. When the beautician swung my chair around to face the mirror again and asked, "What do you think?" all I said was, "Looks good," even though it didn't. (A kind of sphinx hairdo, to be honest—a wedge shape at either side.)

"Will this be a big wedding?" she asked as she lifted my wrap off.

But I could tell she'd asked only to fill the silence, so I just said, "Nope," and handed her my credit card.

Then I heard my ringtone as I was signing my receipt, so I made a big show of rushing to the door as I pulled my phone from my purse. Oh! Debbie. Out on the sidewalk I said, "Hello?"

"Mom?"

"Hi, Deb. Have you finished your Day of Beauty?"

"No, no! Goodness. We've only just gotten to our pedicures. But I wanted to call and tell you that Dad has arrived way early."

"I know that," I said.

"And he has a cat with him."

"I know that."

"You know?"

"He came to the house," I said. "I just happened to be home because . . . and he showed up with his cat, wanting to stay in my guest room."

"Great! Because no way can he stay with me. Kenneth's allergic to cats."

"But *I* don't want him!"

"It'll only be for one night. Or two at the most, depending on how late things run tomorrow."

"Two! He was planning to stay at your place on your actual *wedding night?*"

"So?" Debbie said.

I knew that challenging tone of hers. I backed off a bit. "At any rate, now it's me who's got him," I said. "Aren't I lucky."

"It won't be so bad."

"But you know how he always takes a place over. Little messes everywhere he goes. Besides which, don't forget he's turned vegan."

"He has?"

"It was his New Year's resolution this year, remember?"

"Well, what of it? You're not supplying his meals, after all. Today there's the rehearsal dinner and tomorrow the... Wait, did he mention he was vegan when he RSVPed for tomorrow?"

"How would I know?" I asked.

I was getting into my car. It had heated up enough inside so that I could feel my two fans of hair wilting on either side of my face, which was probably for the best.

"In any case," I said, "he'll need lunch today, and then breakfast and lunch tomorrow, and maybe breakfast the day after, even, if he's really not planning to leave straight after the wedding."

"Never mind; he won't expect you to cook for him."

"Sure, he'll be all 'Don't go to any trouble for *me*,' and 'I'll just find something on my own; never mind,' which of course means he'll haul out every possible item from my fridge and then leave it all on the kitchen counter."

Debbie stayed silent, which was her usual tactic whenever I complained to her about Max. I made myself shut up. I said, "Anyway. How's your Day of Beauty going?"

"Going well," she said cheerfully.

"I just got my hair done myself," I told her. "I took the day off, in fact. I have nothing else to do for the entire rest of the day."

"Well, good," she said briskly. "See you this evening!" And she hung up.

I looked at my phone for a moment, and then I put it back in my purse. Poking forth from my billfold, I happened to notice, was the freebie I'd been handed with my receipt at the beauty parlor—a sample-size foil packet. I plucked it out to examine it. *Remarkable Rouge Co.*, it read. *Instant youthful*

Then I heard my ringtone as I was signing my receipt, so I made a big show of rushing to the door as I pulled my phone from my purse. Oh! Debbie. Out on the sidewalk I said, "Hello?"

"Mom?"

"Hi, Deb. Have you finished your Day of Beauty?"

"No, no! Goodness. We've only just gotten to our pedicures. But I wanted to call and tell you that Dad has arrived way early."

"I know that," I said.

"And he has a cat with him."

"I know that."

"You know?"

"He came to the house," I said. "I just happened to be home because . . . and he showed up with his cat, wanting to stay in my guest room."

"Great! Because no way can he stay with me. Kenneth's allergic to cats."

"But *I* don't want him!"

"It'll only be for one night. Or two at the most, depending on how late things run tomorrow."

"Two! He was planning to stay at your place on your actual *wedding night?*"

"So?" Debbie said.

I knew that challenging tone of hers. I backed off a bit. "At any rate, now it's me who's got him," I said. "Aren't I lucky."

"It won't be so bad."

"But you know how he always takes a place over. Little messes everywhere he goes. Besides which, don't forget he's turned vegan."

"He has?"

"It was his New Year's resolution this year, remember?"

"Well, what of it? You're not supplying his meals, after all. Today there's the rehearsal dinner and tomorrow the . . . Wait, did he mention he was vegan when he RSVPed for tomorrow?"

"How would I know?" I asked.

I was getting into my car. It had heated up enough inside so that I could feel my two fans of hair wilting on either side of my face, which was probably for the best.

"In any case," I said, "he'll need lunch today, and then breakfast and lunch tomorrow, and maybe breakfast the day after, even, if he's really not planning to leave straight after the wedding."

"Never mind; he won't expect you to cook for him."

"Sure, he'll be all 'Don't go to any trouble for *me*,' and 'I'll just find something on my own; never mind,' which of course means he'll haul out every possible item from my fridge and then leave it all on the kitchen counter."

Debbie stayed silent, which was her usual tactic whenever I complained to her about Max. I made myself shut up. I said, "Anyway. How's your Day of Beauty going?"

"Going well," she said cheerfully.

"I just got my hair done myself," I told her. "I took the day off, in fact. I have nothing else to do for the entire rest of the day."

"Well, good," she said briskly. "See you this evening!" And she hung up.

I looked at my phone for a moment, and then I put it back in my purse. Poking forth from my billfold, I happened to notice, was the freebie I'd been handed with my receipt at the beauty parlor—a sample-size foil packet. I plucked it out to examine it. *Remarkable Rouge Co.*, it read. *Instant youthful glow for cheekbones and eyelids.* I tore the notch at one corner and took a sniff of the contents. Kind of fruity-smelling; not what I would have chosen. I squeezed a bit on my fingertip and dabbed one cheekbone, but when I checked in the rearview mirror it looked as if I'd merely been careless with some mayonnaise. I wiped it off. It seemed there were tears in my eyes, but I couldn't say why. I dropped the packet back in my purse and started the car.

I hadn't given Max enough credit, it turned out. When I got home I found he'd fixed a nice lunch for both of us: grilled cheese sandwiches and a salad, with almost no mess to be seen. He waited until I actually walked into the kitchen before he lit the burner under the grill pan, but the table was already set and the salad was already dressed. "Grilled cheese?" I asked. "I thought you'd gone vegan."

"Not all *that* vegan," he said. "I guess more what you'd call vegetarian."

"Oh, good," I said.

I draped my rehearsal dress over one chair and sat down in another. I was thinking he might comment on my new hairdo, but when he turned from the stove to look at me he said, "Gaily-girl! Have you been crying?"

"What? No!" I said.

"It looks to me as if—"

"I don't know why you ever went vegan in the first place," I told him. "We human beings are not a naturally vegan species."

"Well, I'm sixty-five years old, remember," he said. He turned back to the stove. "My doctor says I should start living more proactively. He's got me walking two miles every morning and cutting down on my salt and doing geckos."

"Doing what?"

"Like, when you tighten all your pelvic floor muscles and then relax them," he said.

"Oh, *Kegels*," I said.

"Right. Kegels." He slid his spatula under a sandwich and gave it a flip. "Tighten your pelvic muscles three seconds and then relax three seconds, tighten and then—"

"In fact, I've just now done one," I announced.

"Yes, me too," he said.

We both snickered.

I'd forgotten how cozy it felt sometimes, hanging out with Max.

But then he had to go and point his spatula at me, very instructive and all-knowing. "Of *course* you've been crying," he said. "You're losing your only daughter. It's completely understandable."

"I'm not losing her!"

"In a manner of speaking, you are," he said.

"No, not even in a manner of speaking. She'll be twenty minutes away from me, exactly like before, and she's adding a guy to our family whom I get along with very well."

"But he'll use up all her time," Max said. "And he'll expect her to come to *his* family for holidays and such and you'll practically never see her again."

"You are so absurd," I said. Then I said, "Where's the cat?"

"Wasn't she in the living room?"

"Not that I noticed."

"One thing I was thinking," he said. He was sliding a sandwich onto my plate. "If you *do* decide to adopt her, I believe they have preventive injections these days for severely allergic people. In case you're worried that Kenneth can't visit here anymore."

"It hadn't so much as crossed my mind," I told him. "There's no way I'm going to adopt her, Max. Put that notion out of your head. But since she's here at the moment, what does that mean for the next time Kenneth comes to dinner or something? How long does dander hang around, actually?"

"I have no idea," Max said. It didn't seem to worry him much. He dished out his own sandwich and then returned the grill pan to the stove and sat down across from me.

"Dander," I said thoughtfully. "It's such a peculiar word, when you consider it."

He helped himself to the salad and then passed the bowl to me.

"One of those words where if you say it several times in a row, you start wondering if you made it up," I said.

"Although there *could* be a little problem with their kids," he said.

"Kids?"

"If they inherit his allergy."

"Then I'd just have to have nothing to do with them, I guess."

He stared at me. He seemed to think I was serious.

"So here's the drill," I told him. "We're meeting at the church at five thirty. Debbie and Kenneth, and Kenneth's parents, and Elizabeth, his sister. She's the maid of honor. And then two bridesmaids, Bitsy Taylor and Caroline Byrd. You remember them from Debbie's college days."

"I do?" Max asked.

"You do. And Kenneth's uncle—Jason? Jonas?—is best man,

and two of Kenneth's friends are ushers but I don't know their names; and you and me and my mom."

"Your mom's going to be in the wedding?"

"No, but she doesn't want to miss anything."

"That's quite a crowd," Max said. He took a bite of his sandwich.

"Not really, compared to most weddings," I said. "And it won't be super-formal. Debbie's thirty-three years old, after all."

"So? Nowadays, that's nothing."

"Right, but you can see how all the usual froufrou would be kind of beside the point, at this stage. So no puffy long dress with a train or whatever, and no flower girls and no choir. Just the church organist playing something or other unnoticeable to fill the airwaves, I gather."

"Am I supposed to walk her down the aisle?"

"The organist?"

"Debbie. Like, she and I walk down the aisle arm in arm and I give her away?"

"No, no, she's walking down the aisle alone. Kenneth will be waiting for her at the altar, next to Reverend What's-his-name, and you and I will be sitting in the front pew, on the left—the bride's side. Kenneth's parents will sit on the right."

"Are Kenneth's parents still married to each other?"

"Why, yes."

"But even though you and I are *not* still married, we'll be sitting together?"

"Unless you object, for some reason."

"No, I was just thinking that people might misunderstand," he said.

"Misunderstand in what way?" I asked.

"Won't they think we're still married, too?"

You had to wonder, sometimes, how on earth Max's mind worked.

"I couldn't tell you what they'll think," I said. "In any case, the way the minister's going to word it is, 'Who is it who blesses this couple's choice?' *Not* 'Who gives this woman away?' You see the difference: she isn't really ours to give. And then you and I stand up and say, in unison, 'We do.'"

"How do we work that?"

"Work what?"

"How do we make sure we're in unison?"

"Um..."

"I think we should hold hands," Max said.

"Hold hands?"

"That way, I can give your hand a squeeze so that both of us begin speaking at exactly the same instant."

"Fine," I said.

"Although people really *will* think we're still married if we're holding hands."

"Max," I said, "the guest list for this wedding is shorter than for some dinners I've been to. Everybody attending knows our entire family history."

"Kenneth's family doesn't. I've never even met them."

"I'm sure by now they've been brought up to speed," I said. "This salad is delicious, by the way."

"Why, thank you. I was impressed that you had hearts of palm in your cupboard."

"I did?"

"Shoot," he said. "Maybe I should have checked the expiration date."

"You know I don't believe in expiration dates," I told him.

"Remember *our* wedding?" he asked.

"We didn't have a wedding," I said.

"We most certainly did. We had a lovely private ceremony in city hall."

"Ah, yes. You wore jeans and a dashiki," I said.

"*You* wore all black, with black tights."

I polished off the last of my sandwich and wiped my fingers on my napkin. "So, the rehearsal dinner itself," I said, "is not what you'd call a formal occasion. I mean, it's in a nice restaurant, but there won't be any toasts or speeches or anything like that."

"They're saving that kind of thing for tomorrow," Max suggested. "For the banquet after the wedding."

"Not so much even then," I said. "You know our Debbie. She's been pretty good at reining things in."

Max chuckled approvingly.

I said, "Did you show the cat where you were putting her litter box?"

"I'm sure she'll figure it out," he said.

I glanced toward the powder room. "With the door shut?" I asked him.

"Oh," he said.

I stood up and went to open the door. The litter box sat next to the toilet, filled with kitty litter but pristine. I continued into the living room. "Cat?" I called.

Max followed me, saying, "Kitty-kitty-kitty?"

I climbed the stairs and went into the guest room, figuring that that would at least smell familiar to her, since Max had stowed his things there. No sign of her, though. So next I tried my own room, where I found her asleep on my pillow. She raised her head and stared at me. "Aww," Max said. "Look at that: she deliberately chose your bed."

I scooped her up and handed her to him. "Show her where her litter box is," I ordered.

"Sure thing! Come with me, sweetie-pie," he told the cat.

"And for God's sake, leave the powder room door open!"

"Will do," he said. He left.

I walked over to the bureau and checked my hairdo in the mirror. It was less sphinxlike, but it still stood out a bit on either side. So I crossed the hall to the bathroom and dampened my comb and ran it through my hair till it hung vertically. My face looked perfectly normal, as far as I could tell. I don't know why Max thought I'd been crying.

⁓⁓

Black turtleneck and a black skirt and black tights; that's what I wore to my wedding.

How we met was, he moved into the house where I'd been living with three fellow teachers. At first I wasn't all that welcoming. He was the only male in our group, for one thing—sprung on us by Polly Soames when she moved out to get married. Plus, he brought along a rambunctious dog that he hadn't asked permission for, and he generated hillocks of clutter wherever he sat, and he played his radio too loudly and stayed up too long after the rest of us had gone to bed. (He was working then at an after-school center for inner-city children, which meant he kept different hours from us.) Also, he was forever nibbling at things in the fridge that didn't belong to him. One time he consumed the entire contents of a jar labeled

CAUTION—SEWAGE SAMPLE because he figured it was just a ruse to protect somebody's chicken soup. Actually, it *was* just a ruse, but wouldn't you think he'd have been embarrassed that the owner felt a ruse was necessary? He ate the last piece of cake that Julie Sears's mother had baked her for her birthday. He cadged Priscilla Oakley's umbrella from the hall closet on a rainy day and then, to make matters worse, left it by accident in his dentist's waiting room.

Boundaries; that was his problem. He lacked boundaries.

I myself was all about boundaries.

Still, I couldn't help liking him. He was exceptionally kindhearted with both animals and children, and he had a sweet, trusting face—beardless, back then—and he was happy to share anything in his possession, anything at all. Besides which, he thought I'd hung the moon. It's hard to resist someone who thinks you hung the moon. "Oh, Gail is reading that too!" he would say to an acquaintance. "Gail reads *everything*; you wouldn't believe how much." Or, "You majored in Spanish? You should hear Gail's Spanish; she rolls her *r*s like a native." He always laughed at my jokes and he loved to hear my stories about my students. It bowled him over that I never wore makeup.

When we first met, I was dating someone, but I wasn't all that serious about him; and meanwhile Max and I were falling into one of those half-flirtatious friendships that could become more than a friendship if one of us made the slightest move in that direction. We were kind of teetering, you might say. Things were hanging in the balance.

I had been teaching in a private school on a sort of provisional basis, filling in for a teacher who'd taken a year off to have a baby and then, as it happened, another year after that.

It was implied that once she returned I might be switched to something more permanent; but no; when she announced the next spring that she'd be coming back in September, I was let go after all. I was devastated. "I thought I'd been doing such a good job!" I told Max, and he said, "You *were* doing a good job. It's not your fault there wasn't an opening," and other such things that friends tell each other. He wanted me to apply at his center, but I had set my heart on teaching; nothing but.

While I was frittering my summer away hoping for another opening, he and I went to a lot of movies together, a lot of cafés and free concerts, and we grew steadily more comfortable with each other. Leaving a café, for instance, he might casually sling an arm across my shoulders; and during a horror film I might grab his hand for reassurance. Then in the fall— I'd been hired by a school in Baltimore County by then, and really should have looked for a new place to live but somehow did not—we went on a picnic out in Hunt Valley. It was Max's idea. He must have done some scouting beforehand, because he drove us directly to a giant field, a vast stretch of wheat or oats or barley or something, very beautiful and golden. Of course we brought his dog along—Barbara, her name was; she was mostly black Labrador—and she kept racing ahead and then wheeling and racing back to us in sheer exuberance. She would stop short in front of me and jump up to place her paws on my shoulders, sending out warm puffs of dog breath. "I ought to be jealous," Max said, and then, speaking to Barbara, "At least you've got good taste," and she gave a yip and dashed off again. Max was carrying a Pantry Pride grocery bag with our lunch in it, and I remember that he set the bag down on a patch of grass under an oak tree before he turned around and cupped my face in both of his hands. He looked at me soberly for a moment, and then he leaned forward to kiss me on the lips. It was both unexpected and entirely natural-feeling. I hesitated for one brief second and then I kissed him back.

But even after that it was not a done deal, not by any means. I had to be won again and again, re-won several times over. I would wake some mornings—wake in Max's bed, by then—and ask myself what I thought I was doing. I would rehearse how I would explain to him that we had no future together.

Partly, this was because he often struck me as a case of arrested development. A man nearing thirty, still renting a room in a houseful of single women! Still experimenting with new professions, new avenues of enthusiasm! Why, merely getting through college had taken him six years, because he'd kept switching majors. Also, he was just as annoying a housemate as he'd ever been. No amount of nagging from the rest of us altered his behavior in the slightest.

And yet...

I think he knew all that. I mean, he knew I blew hot and cold about him. He had this way of vanishing whenever I found him impossible, and then drifting into view again when he sensed I was starting to miss him. Once, I remember, I got so mad at him that I went to my parents' house for the weekend without telling him I was going. He'd read my private mail, was why. I had come home from work to find him chuckling over a letter I'd left on top of my bureau, and even though it was merely a chatty, catching-up kind of letter from my old college roommate I was furious, and told him so, and he couldn't understand why. "It was lying there out of its envelope!" he said. "And it was only about this blind date she'd had! If that was such a secret, why did you leave it out for all and sundry to see?" I didn't bother answering that; I just left. Took my car keys and left. Stayed with my parents all weekend, and then on Sunday afternoon, when I was beginning to wonder how I should behave after I returned, he came to fetch me. Apparently he'd phoned my mother and she had told him yes, I was there, even though she knew the reason I was there. Mom was crazy about Max. So was my dad. (Dad asked how he could *not* be crazy about a guy who treated me like a queen.) So Max showed up at the house unannounced, bringing along Barbara, and when Barbara saw me she got down on her stomach and wriggled toward me, all whiny and obsequious and wagging her tail, even though she was not the one who had wronged me; and my parents stood behind me saying, "Aww!" and "Look at her, Gail! How can you resist her?"—meaning, of course, how could I resist Max, who had not uttered so much as a "Sorry" and was just standing there smiling hopefully with his arms folded across his chest. I don't know who I was madder at: him or my parents. I was even mad at Barbara, a little, because she had no business making me feel so grouchy, and so guilty about feeling grouchy, and so lovingly entrapped.

When we got married, the following January, we did it all in a rush. Was it Max who decided that, figuring he should grab his chance before I changed my mind? Or was it me, in fact, for the very same reason—scared of my own fickle nature? Well, maybe both, a little. In any case, we chose a Friday afternoon and we drove downtown by ourselves and parked in a public lot. Several inches of snow were supposed to fall before evening, so all the other parked cars were sticking their windshield wipers straight up like soldiers in surrender, and the city had a startled, suspenseful feeling as if it were holding its breath.

But I've never been the type to play back scenes from my past. At most a single unexpected moment might pop up—

Debbie taking her first steps and then abruptly plopping her plastic-coated bottom down; my father whistling "The Tennessee Waltz" as he tinkered with a leaky faucet—and I would think, *Oh, that.* Or, *Oh! That!* if it really took me by surprise. And then I turned my eyes away from it and thought about something else.

⁂

We had several hours to fill before the rehearsal, so Max went off to take a nap. (He'd always made kind of a hobby of naps.) Meanwhile I tidied up in the kitchen, and leafed through that morning's mail, and started a load of laundry. I considered running the vacuum cleaner, but that seemed rude when Max was sleeping. Also, it might alarm the cat. The cat! I went upstairs to find her. She was curled up again on my pillow; she raised her head and gave a questioning mew and stretched out her front legs luxuriously. So I risked gathering her up and carrying her downstairs. She didn't object, just gave a huge yawn when I settled with her in the armchair. "So, Madam Cat," I said, "what's your story, hmm?" She fitted herself to the shape of my lap and went back to sleep.

I had meant it when I said I didn't want a cat. I didn't even want a houseplant; I had reached the stage of life when I was done with caretaking. But for the moment, I enjoyed scritching her behind her ears, and smoothing her velvety front paws, and admiring her sprouts of eyebrows. I fell into a sort of trance, in fact, so that when the front door suddenly opened I was nearly as startled as the cat was.

It was only Debbie, though. She looked like a movie star. She was wearing her usual weekend outfit—jeans and a tank top—but she was stunningly made up, with bright red lipstick and soft pink blush and blue-gray eye shadow that brought out the aqua blue of her eyes, and her hair hung to her shoulders in a straight blond sheet. "Glamour puss!" I said.

I had never expected that a daughter of mine would look like Debbie. When I found out I'd be having a girl I had pictured . . . oh, a small, pale, bony girl with a watchful stillness to her, and she might wear horn-rimmed glasses and in her teens she wouldn't date much and her friends would address her as "Deborah." But children veer out from their parents like so many explorers in the wilderness, I've learned. They're not mere duplicates of them. I was fascinated by that. I was fascinated by everything about her. "You should have a pack of photographers hounding you," I said now.

But she just said, "Huh." She didn't comment on the cat. She sat down in a heap on the couch and grabbed the nearest cushion and hugged it close to her chest like a child with a favorite stuffed animal.

"What's wrong?" I asked her.

"Nothing's wrong."

"Is it the weather?" I asked. Because she'd been fretting for the past several days about the long-term forecast, and I did hear rain on the roof now.

But she shook her head.

Then she said, "Where's Dad?"

"Oh, he's—"

"Here I am," Max said. He was padding down the stairs in his stocking feet, alert as always to any sign of Debbie's presence. "Whoa!" he said as he came closer. "Miss Universe!" He bent to set an arm gingerly around her neck and give her a kiss. "How was your Ladies' Day or whatever?"

"It was good," she said.

"Everyone have a nice time?"

"Oh, yes," she said. Max gave her a sharp look and then sat down on the couch too, but at a little more of a distance than he might have ordinarily. The cat, meanwhile, disappeared—just melted away, as cats do.

There was a silence. Then Max said, "What."

"What," Debbie repeated.

"Is something wrong?"

"What could be wrong?" she asked him.

Then she buried her face in the cushion and her shoulders started shaking.

I said, "Debbie?"

Max said, "Hon?"

"Debbie, *tell* us," I commanded.

She raised her head and dabbed at her nose with the back of her hand. Her face was entirely wet with tears.

"Is it Kenneth?" I asked her. "Is it something to do with the wedding?" Then I said, "You've changed your mind."

She made a lunge toward the box on the coffee table and snatched a Kleenex and blotted her eyes.

"You know you're always free to back out," I told her. "Even at the last minute! Even walking down the aisle!"

Max stirred uneasily and said, "Well, now . . ."

"Is that it?" I asked her. "You don't want to marry him anymore?"

"I *can't* marry him," she said.

From the way she worded it, my first thought was that she meant she wasn't allowed to marry him. She was married to someone else, perhaps, or she'd run into some bizarre legal snafu. "Who says?" I asked her.

She said, "I was sitting at the manicure station, okay? I was about to get my nails done. And Liz was sitting next to me."

"Liz," I said, at a loss.

"Elizabeth, his sister, Mom. Waiting to get *her* nails done. Pay attention."

"Okay..."

"She says to me, 'Debbie, I am so, so glad Kenneth straightened things out with you before the wedding. I warned him,' she said, 'I said, "Kenny, you cannot embark on a marriage with this left unspoken between you," and he was like, "Oh, sure; oh, sure," and kept putting it off, and so finally I said, "Look here, Kenneth. If you don't tell her, I will," I said. So he was, like—"

This was becoming a bit hard to follow. I said, "So, wait—"

"And I was just baffled," Debbie said. "I said, 'Tell me what, Liz?' And she got very quiet, and then she said, 'Uh-oh.'"

"Tell you what?" I asked.

"Turns out he slept with Carla Schmidt while I was at my college reunion last month."

"Who is Carla Schmidt?" Max asked.

I just gave him a look, and Debbie, needless to say, didn't bother answering. "One and a half days I was gone," she told me. "Not even a whole weekend!"

I said, "But—"

I couldn't get my brain around it. I felt I'd been kicked in the chest. *Debbie's* Kenneth? But he loved her! I said, "I just can't see that happening."

"Then Liz of course was all, 'Oops, I didn't mean to—' and, 'Oh, God, I thought he'd told you! He swore to me he'd told you!'"

"But how would Elizabeth even know about it?" I asked.

"Did he actually discuss it with her? Why would he choose to do that?"

"Right," Max said. He was nodding.

"He didn't *choose*," Debbie said. "She confronted him, straight out, and he couldn't deny it. The minute I heard her say the words, it was like something just clicked in my mind, you know?"

"Oh," I said.

"But . . . so, let's suppose it's true," Max told her. "Merely *suppose*, I'm saying. Let's put this in perspective. I mean, these things happen, Deb. Pre-wedding jitters, last-minute-fling sort of thing . . . It's not the end of the world."

Debbie wheeled on him. She said, "I might have known you'd say that! Men just think these things are normal, just in the normal course of events." And then she turned to me and said, "I'll have to call off the wedding, of course."

"Yes . . . of course," I said. I cleared my throat. My voice didn't seem to be working properly.

She said, "Could you please be the one to phone the minister? If I have to do it myself I'm worried I might start crying."

"Certainly," I said.

"Wait," Max said.

"And then also the guests," Debbie said. "Well, the guests on *our* side, at least. I don't care who gets in touch with their side. Let's not even bother with their side. They can just all show up and wonder what could have gone wrong."

"Would you two *listen* a minute?" Max asked.

This time, both of us turned on him. "Max," I said, "we are talking about someone she's been planning to spend her life with. Someone she needs to trust completely, she needs to believe in wholeheartedly until the end of her days. And now we hear he can't be relied on for even as long as a college reunion?"

"All I'm saying is—"

"Forget it, Mom," Debbie told me. "Apparently we're dealing with one of those gender-gap things."

"Now, that's just plain insulting," Max said. "I refuse to stand in for your notion of a male chauvinist."

"I didn't say—"

"Deborah Jean Baines," Max said. "Please hear me out for one minute."

Debbie grew very attentive, but in an ostentatious way. She sat up extra straight and fixed him with a wide stare.

"I suggest you delay this decision until you've talked with Kenneth," he told her. "Is he at work still? What time does he get off work? Please just go see him and find out what he has to say about this. There may be some explanation that puts everything in a whole different light."

"What possible explanation do you imagine that could be?" Debbie asked him.

"That's my point. We don't *know* what it could be, do we?"

"Mom?" Debbie said, turning to me. "You see my side of this, don't you?"

"I certainly do," I said.

"All I'm asking," Max told her, "is let the guy speak for himself. Is that so unreasonable?"

"I'm beginning to get the picture here," she said.

"What picture?" he asked.

She looked from him to me, and then she said, "Never mind."

"What picture are you talking about?"

She turned back to Max. "Fine," she told him. "I'll go talk to him. I'll do it as a special favor to you, Dad, since you seem to think it's so important."

"Thanks, hon," Max said cheerfully. Whatever her nuances were, he seemed content to let them pass right over his head.

And he did have a point. Of course she should listen to Kenneth's side of things. Still, though, I felt almost regretful when she stood up and slammed out of the house. There was something weirdly satisfying in the image of all those guests just sitting in church wondering.

It was nearly four o'clock by then, and I very much doubted that Kenneth would be working his normal hours today. (He had something to do with the legal side of a real estate company—not what I supposed to be a punching-the-clock type of job.) I pictured that Debbie might go directly from my house to his apartment, in which case she'd be nearing Charles Street by now, and now she'd be turning south. Probably Max was thinking along the same lines, because instead of heading back upstairs to put his shoes on he started drifting aimlessly around the living room, first tweaking the curtain to peer outside, then bending over the coffee table to inspect the front page of the newspaper, and finally wandering out to the kitchen, where I heard him open the fridge door and close it again. When he came back to the living room, he said, "What do you think she meant when she said, 'I'm beginning to get the picture'?"

"I couldn't tell you," I said. Then I said, "You don't really believe Kenneth can explain his way out of this, do you?"

"I'm suspending judgment," Max said.

I looked at the clock on the bookshelf. I said, "If she doesn't report back soon, we're going to have to go ahead and start dressing for the rehearsal."

"We should probably dress anyhow," Max said. "Because in either case, we'll need to show up at the church. Either to attend or to cancel, one or the other."

"Maybe she won't *ever* report back," I said. "Maybe she'll be too devastated to let us know, even; maybe she'll just go home to her place and crawl into bed."

Max thought this over. Then he said, "How's this: if we still haven't heard from her by the time we're dressed, we'll phone her."

"Okay," I said. But I went on sitting in the armchair.

He said, "Coming?"

Very slowly, I stood up. I said, "You know what I'm scared of?"

"What?"

"I'm scared she'll call and say yes, he admitted it, but she's going to marry him anyhow."

"In that case, we'll say, 'Fine, hon. That's your own personal business.'"

I didn't bother arguing with that. I was too irritated. I hated when Max acted so forbearing and holier-than-thou.

At any rate, we went off to our separate rooms to get dressed. All Max had to do was change into a collared shirt and put on his shoes and his sports coat, so he was back downstairs before I was. I could hear him talking as I descended; he was speaking into his cell phone. "Sure thing!" he was saying. "See you in a jiff!" and then he hung up.

"She said she'll meet us at the church," he told me.

I fixed him with a look and waited.

"She said Kenneth explained everything. His sister had it all wrong."

"In what way did she have it wrong?" I asked.

"It turns out this Carla got food poisoning," he said. "Everybody was at some party, Kenneth and his sister and I don't know who-all from their high school days, and Carla felt sick and so he drove her home and stayed to feed her ice chips until she felt better. When he never came back to the party his sister just jumped to conclusions, he said. Besides which, she was miffed because she'd been counting on him for a ride and now she had to fend for herself."

I waited until he met my eyes, which took him longer than it should have. "And you believe that," I said.

"Why, yes, if Debbie does."

"You don't have any doubts."

"No, indeed," he said.

Max never used the word 'indeed.'

"Well, I personally do not believe it," I told him.

"Okay," he said, levelly.

"Just look at the way Debbie put it when she was talking to us before," I said. "'Something clicked in my mind,' she told us. *You* know that feeling, right?"

"Not really," Max said.

"And no matter how miffed Elizabeth was, would she really go that far to get even? Just because Kenneth didn't give her a ride home?"

"You never know," he said.

"Plus, that makes too many explanations. You should always be suspicious when someone gives you too many explanations."

"Unless he actually *has* that many."

Well, now he was just being stubborn. I gave up; I went to the closet for my purse. "Also," I said, "I thought you weren't going to phone Deb until we both got back downstairs."

"I didn't," he said. "She's the one who phoned *me*."

I considered that.

"But anyhow!" he said. "Are we taking your car, or mine?"

"Yours, if it's all right with you."

"It's fine."

"And we're picking up my mother on the way," I said. "But let's not tell her about the Kenneth business, okay?"

"No, of course not," Max said.

I'd been scared of the wrong thing, it turned out. Not that Debbie would marry Kenneth even after he'd betrayed her, but that she would take his word for it when he claimed he hadn't.

My mother was waiting out front when we pulled up, but she didn't know it was us because she was watching for my Corolla. I had to roll down my window and call, "Mom!" before she realized. Then she came over and peered in. "Why, Max," she said when she saw him.

"Hi, there," he said.

"He's going to have to stay at my house tonight because he brought a cat," I told her.

"A cat," she said.

"And Kenneth is allergic to cats."

She still looked a bit uncertain, but she opened the rear door and got in. She was a lot more dressed up than I was—blue-and-white-flowered silk, high heels, patent leather purse—but in her old age she'd grown scrawny and her dress hung on her like a sack. (She wouldn't buy any smaller-size clothes because she claimed she'd never get her money's worth out of them, meaning she expected to die at any moment, although she was perfectly healthy.) It always made me feel a little sad these days to see her.

She was in high spirits, though. "Isn't this exciting?" she asked as she shut her door.

"Very exciting," I said.

"How did Debbie's spa day go?"

"It went fine," I said.

"Women have all the fun, don't they? I bet Kenneth and *his* friends didn't have a spa day!"

"Nope," I said. "Kenneth went to work as usual, I believe."

Mom gave a little bounce in order to smooth her skirt beneath her. "And it's stopped raining!" she said.

"Mm-hmm."

I wasn't rising to the occasion sufficiently; I was aware of that. Maybe Max was, too, because once we were on the road again he glanced at her in the rearview mirror and said, "How've you been, Joyce?"

"Very well, thank you," she said.

He used to call her "Mom." Then after the divorce she said, "I guess 'Mom' is kind of misleading now, don't you think?" Probably she meant he should go back to "Mrs. Simmons," but when he switched to "Joyce" she didn't correct him. She was in new territory, after all; we'd never had a divorce in our family. She really didn't know how to handle it. And I was not much help. She kept asking me *why*. She said, "I just don't understand what could have gone wrong," but all I said was, "Oh, you know how these things are. No one outside of a marriage has the least notion what's going on inside." I did try to make it clear that Max should not be blamed. Even so, though, she developed a polite but distant tone with him on the rare occasions she saw him. Now she said, "You've done something to your hair, I think," and her shift of focus away from Max was so abrupt that he said, "No . . ." before he realized it was me she was addressing.

"I got a kind of comb-out," I said.

"Very nice, dear."

On other weekdays we'd have had rush hour to deal with, but Baltimoreans leave work early on Fridays and the streets were all but empty. The church wasn't far, anyhow. (It was Kenneth's parents' church. Our own family didn't have one.) "I hope we're not late," my mother said, gazing out at a bus stop where a single old man sat waiting. "They might decide to start without us."

Max said, "No, no, we're the ones doing the starting. Have to give the bride away, don't you know."

"They still give brides away?"

"In a manner of speaking."

The church parking lot held just a few cars, widely scattered, but while we were getting out of Max's car another one pulled up next to us, a convertible with a young man at the wheel, no doubt one of the ushers, and he joined us as we walked toward the church. "Hello there," he said. "Dave Lewis," and Max said, "Gail and Max Baines. And this is Gail's mother, Joyce Simmons."

"Ah, yes, you two are giving the bride away."

I said, "Well, not—" but Max overrode me. "Right," he said.

We climbed the front steps and entered the foyer, which smelled like furniture polish. The church interior was small but elegant, with an elaborately carved pulpit up front made of some dark wood. The pulpit was where the action was. Everyone stood clustered around it, listening to the minister say something about the organist. But Debbie was the one I was looking for. I found her standing at the edge of the group, between Kenneth and his parents. Even from behind I could tell she'd pulled herself together. Every hair was in place, and she had traded her jeans for a long full skirt. One of Kenneth's hands was resting possessively on her waist, but she kept a bit separate from him, I thought. Or maybe I was imagining that.

It was Kenneth who spotted us first. He turned and said, "*There* they are!" and then Debbie turned too and said, "Oh, good," and they came over to us. No one would have guessed Debbie had recently been crying. And Kenneth seemed very much his normal, sunny self—a pleasant-faced, calm young man with a shock of straight blond hair falling over his forehead and an engagingly lopsided smile. He said, "Hi there, Deb's Gram," which was how he always addressed my mother, and he pecked her on the cheek and gave me a hug. I stayed rigid and merely endured it, but I don't think he noticed.

"I just want to warn you," Max was telling him, "I may be contagious."

"Contagious?" Kenneth asked.

"Got a little cat dander on me."

"Yes, I heard," Kenneth said, but he didn't sound alarmed. "Well, I did bring my inhaler, if worse comes to worst."

"Inhaler!" Max and I said in a single voice.

Kenneth blinked.

"Kenneth actually went to work today," Debbie told us. "Can you believe it?"

This wasn't news to us, of course. It was merely her way of

claiming him, making sure we understood that she was still in his corner; so I said, dutifully, "*Oh*, my," and shook my head.

Then here came his mother, dark-haired and stylish and looking way younger than me. "Good evening, Gail!" she said. "And this must be Max! Hello, Max, so nice to meet you, finally. I'm Sophie, and this is Rupert," because Kenneth's father was close behind her. It was his fair coloring that Kenneth had inherited, but Rupert had a plumper face and the beginnings of a paunch. "And Elizabeth," Sophie added. "Kenneth's sister."

"Ah," I said.

Elizabeth turned out to resemble her father, soft-cheeked and a bit overweight. She hadn't made the same effort with her outfit as the others; she wore loose brown slacks and a casual overblouse. Was it because her heart wasn't really in this wedding? I felt distinctly hostile toward her. Even though I believed her story, it seemed that in some way she had *caused* the story, merely by reporting it. And her mother: Did she believe it too? Had she even heard about it? No, I wouldn't think so. She was holding both of Mom's hands in her own and, "My goodness, Joyce!" she was saying. "You look like a bride yourself!" My mother raised her eyebrows. Everything Sophie said, as a rule, was about three degrees too vivacious. It seemed that she lived on some other level than ours, someplace louder and more brightly lit.

But we were creating a distraction, so we broke off and headed up front with Sophie to be introduced to the minister. Reverend Gregory, his name was. He seemed too elegant for a minister, with his smartly tailored slacks and the collar of his shirt standing up too deliberately at the rear. "Ah, yes," he said in an almost-English accent, "I'm delighted to meet Deborah's loved ones," and he went on to explain that we'd be doing without the organist this evening, since she was in bed with a migraine, but that she would be with us tomorrow. After that, Sophie turned to address the group as a whole. "I suppose all of you know by now," she said, "that Kenneth and Debbie seem to have something against the notion of a wedding planner. But I've done some research on Google, and there are a few things I'd like to point out." Which she proceeded to do, looking very happy to find herself in charge. Who should signal the start of the processional, for instance; who should stand where, who should say what... She had it all written down on an index card that she pulled from the depths of her purse. I found this a relief, to be honest. Better her than me. I watched at one remove as she debated with herself about where my mother should be seated. With Max and me in the front left pew, perhaps? Or with other relatives one row back, so she wouldn't be left alone when we rose to bless the couple's choice? No, wait. Maybe Mom should join Max and me in the blessing. But here my mother put her foot down. "Certainly not," she said, and then to me, in an undertone, "Where would it all end? With your aunt Tess blessing them too? With random second cousins?" We didn't have any random second cousins that I knew of, but I said, "Good point, Mom. Let's keep it simple."

During all of this, though, I was secretly focused on Debbie. I kept trying to figure out her state of mind. Unfortunately, I could see her face only in profile. When Kenneth murmured something in her ear, I wondered what it meant that she drew away to look at him. When she laughed, I relaxed slightly.

"Nice that she didn't get false eyelashes at that spa place," my mother told me. "What with those gorgeous lashes of her own."

"Yes..."

"Will she just not wash her face till after the wedding, do you suppose?"

"No, a person is coming from Darleen's tomorrow to do it all over again," I said, because I'd asked Debbie the same question.

Then someone behind me tapped my shoulder, and I turned to see a man who could only be Uncle... Jacob? He was lean and high cheekboned with iron-gray hair, clearly from Sophie's side of the family. "Gail?" he said.

"Yes?"

"I'm Jared Johnson. Remember me?"

I gave him a closer look "Jared?" I said.

Of course. I should have recognized him. Jared was who I'd been going out with when I met Max. Except he'd had a full beard back then, and coal-black hair that nearly reached his waist. "My goodness!" I said. He hadn't been half so handsome in those days, at least not that I'd been able to see under all that fur. And he had certainly not worn such a dignified suit.

"I had guessed it might be you," he said. "I've been looking forward to seeing you ever since my sister began talking about the wedding. And... Max, isn't it?"

"Hey there," Max said. I could tell he didn't have a clue who this was.

"So you two ended up married," Jared said. "And divorced, I hear."

"That's right," I said.

"I'm divorced myself," he said. "Married a California gal and moved out west, but now I'm back east. Took an administrative job in College Park."

"And Kenneth's your nephew," I said. "Well, isn't that—"

But then my mother sent me a look, and Max and I faced forward again to hear what Reverend Gregory had to say.

He was clearing his throat in a preparatory way and ruffling through his notes. "As I understand it," he told us, "the bride does not rehearse walking down the aisle ahead of time. It's considered to be bad luck. But might everybody else take their positions, please?"

People started sorting themselves out, Kenneth and Jared heading toward the front of the church while the bridesmaids and the ushers gathered at the rear. I noticed Kenneth's parents settling in the right front pew, so I steered Mom and Max toward our own pew. Mom slid in first, followed by me and then Max. Debbie took a seat next to Max, for the moment. This gave me a chance to lean past Max and ask her, "How're you doing, honey?"

"Doing fine!" she said brightly. "How about you?"

"Oh . . . ," I said.

"It's a nice-looking church, isn't it?"

"Yes, it is," I said, and I gave up and faced forward again.

Max said, suddenly, "Wait. Was that Jared *Johnson*?"

"Now you've got it," I told him.

"I'll be darned," he said, and he cast a glance toward where Jared was standing next to Kenneth.

The two of us had never discussed Jared back in our courting days, probably because I had always been so offhand about him. But now Max seemed slightly unsettled. "Since when did he turn into such an . . . executive type?" he asked.

"No idea," I said.

"Hmph."

Unexpectedly, Reverend Gregory broke into song. "Dah-*dum*-dah-dum!"—the first few notes of "Here Comes the Bride," which I was fairly sure was not what Debbie and Kenneth had chosen for the processional. After a moment of uncertainty, Bitsy took the arm of the usher standing next to her and started walking up the aisle. She kept her free hand clutched in a fist in front of her waist, presumably to imply that she was holding a bouquet. Caroline followed with Dave, the young man we'd met in the parking lot, and then along came Kenneth's sister on her own. I wished, wished, wished that Debbie hadn't chosen Elizabeth to be her maid of honor! Why not Bitsy, for heaven's sake, or Caroline? But maybe that was a matter of politics—cementing the relationship with her future sister-in-law. (And also, perhaps, avoiding the need to choose one equally close friend over the other.) I'd even agreed with her, originally. Never having been all that popular with my own in-laws, I had thought Debbie was starting out on the right foot. But this Elizabeth, with her butter-wouldn't-melt expression and her don't-care outfit!

Debbie was rising now, sidling out of the pew, going up front herself to take her place next to Kenneth. The two of them faced Reverend Gregory, with the maid of honor and the best man on either side. Reverend Gregory set his sheaf of notes upright on the pulpit and tapped them a few times before he laid them flat. Then he raised his head and looked out over his audience. "Dearly beloved," he began, and then he said, "Et cetera, et cetera," and waved a hand dismissively. He turned toward where Max and I were sitting and asked, "Who is it who blesses this couple's choice?"

Max took my hand, and we stood up. When he squeezed my fingers, we started speaking in perfect unison. Except that I said, "We do," and Max said, "Her mother and I do."

I sent him a look, and we dropped hands and sat back down. "Where did *that* come from?" I whispered, and he said, "Sorry, I think that's how they worded it when my niece got married."

Meanwhile, Reverend Gregory was continuing through a string of further "et ceteras," which gave an effect of sloppiness although I could see that he merely intended to keep things fresh for tomorrow. Kenneth and Debbie responded in earnest, though, when the time came. "I do," each said, almost defiantly.

"I now pronounce you et cetera," Reverend Gregory told them. "You may kiss the—sorry, will you two be kissing?"

"Absolutely," Kenneth said.

"You never know, these days," Reverend Gregory said.

Debbie and Kenneth kissed, but just a brief peck. I couldn't tell a thing from it. I was watching, believe me, but to me they seemed perfectly normal.

Were we simply going to carry on as usual, then? As if nothing whatsoever had happened?

Reverend Gregory started singing, "DUM! DUM! Dah-dum-dum-dum-dum"—Mendelssohn's "Wedding March"—and Debbie and Kenneth turned to walk back up the aisle. Jared and Elizabeth fell in behind them, with the other attendants following. When Debbie reached the back of the church, she stopped short and flung something white high in the air and behind her. A pamphlet of some sort, it looked like. "What was *that*?" Mom asked me, and Debbie said, "My bouquet!" even though it wasn't likely that she'd heard Mom's question. "No, dear!" Sophie called, rising from her pew. "The *reception* is where you toss the bouquet! At the tail end of the reception!"

"Oops! Too late," Bitsy said, because she had already stooped to retrieve the pamphlet and she was holding it up triumphantly.

"What *is* this?" Max muttered in my ear. "I thought we weren't going to have a wedding planner."

It could have been much worse, I didn't tell him. He hadn't heard Debbie's day-to-day reports on her struggle to keep things low-key.

And now Sophie was calling out, "Does everyone know where the restaurant is? Does anyone need directions?"

We were going to the Silver Spoon, I'd been told—Sophie and Rupert's decision, since the rehearsal dinner was supposed to be hosted by the groom's parents. The Silver Spoon was considered one of Baltimore's finest restaurants, so my mother clucked approvingly. "Do you suppose they still make their famous crab dip?" she asked as we filed down the aisle.

"I can't imagine why they wouldn't," I said.

"And the waiters still pour the wine from two feet above people's glasses?"

"That I'm less sure of," I told her. "It seems a kind of 1970s thing to do, don't you think?"

"We could hope, though," my mother said.

And we stepped out of the church into rain-washed late-afternoon sunshine, where everyone stood smiling and blinking and looking celebratory.

※※

There would not be any speeches or formalities at this dinner, Sophie had assured me. It would be just your regular restaurant meal, with a minimum number of diners ordering their own food and chattering among themselves at a single long table. Except that Kenneth's father had apparently not been informed of this, and he clinked a fork against his glass as soon as the wine had been poured. (From an unremarkable height, I noticed.) "I'd like to welcome all of you," he told us, "but most especially Deborah. The newest member of the Bailey clan!"

Debbie murmured, "Why, thank you," no doubt assuming that this was the end of it, but no, he had to go on. "The very first time we met her," he said, "I told Sophie I had a feeling that this might be The One. Didn't I, Sofe?"

"You did, dear," she said.

"'You just watch,' I told her. 'We haven't seen the last of that young lady.' This was at Thanksgiving, mind you, a year and a half ago. Debbie brought a pumpkin pie that she had baked from scratch. The most delicious pumpkin pie, and I don't even like pumpkin pie!"

There were chuckles around the table, and my mother, sitting next to me, murmured, "Quite rightly."

"But *this* pie," Rupert went on, "had, I don't know, something fluffy beaten into it, whipped cream or something, so that it wasn't even orange anymore but more like, let's say, beige; and I said to Sophie, I said, 'She wouldn't go to all that trouble if she was just some casual date coming for a free meal. Mark my words,' I said."

Sophie said, "All right, well—"

"And sure enough, just before Valentine's Day—three and a half months later, is all!—Kenneth comes to the house and says, 'What do you think?' and hauls out this diamond ring in a Stieff box. 'I'm going to ask Debbie to marry me,' he says. Well, we were thrilled! Sophie got kind of teary, in fact."

"That's true," Sophie told us. "But anyhow—"

"So here's to you, dear Debbie," Rupert said, and he raised his wineglass. "I hope you'll be very happy in our family!"

The others raised their glasses too, and murmured, and Debbie smiled and said, "Thank you, Rupert," and took a sip from her own glass. But I was sitting diagonally across the table from her, close enough to see that as soon as she set the glass back down, she stopped smiling. And really, the smile had never reached her eyes.

I looked over at Max, two seats away from her, but he was beaming at her fondly and I could tell he suspected nothing.

Who did suspect, though, was Kenneth. He was sitting next to her, focused on her so watchfully that he seemed to be expecting her to give a speech of her own. And even when she didn't, even when she let go of her glass and picked up her menu, he went on studying her.

I'm a worrier; I admit it. I'm always jumping to the worst-case scenario. But this time, I swear I had good reason. I swear he was trying to find out if she had believed his story, and he suspected that she had not. And what's more, he was right: she had not. She was distinctly unhappy.

☙❧

It wasn't till we were driving home that my mother asked what was bothering me. "Bothering me!" I said. "Nothing's bothering me."

"Very well," she said, and she looked pointedly out her side window.

By this time it was dark, and the rain was still in retreat, although Max did turn his wipers on just to whisk the occasional drop away. "Did you enjoy the rehearsal?" he asked Mom.

"Yes, thank you," she said.

"I kind of wish that had been *it*," he said. "Seems like the wedding tomorrow will just be the same thing all over again."

"But with fewer et ceteras," she suggested.

"Let's hope."

"And fancier clothes."

"'Fraid you're right."

"Although that uncle of theirs was quite dressed-up even tonight," she said musingly.

"The uncle and Gail here used to be an item," Max told her.

"They did?" Mom said. "Really?" she asked me.

"We went out a few times," I said.

"I did notice he was all over you."

"He wasn't all over me!"

"Why else would he be so quick to tell you he was no longer married?" she asked. "And then when he practically mowed me down trying to sit next to you at dinner! I had to stick out my pointy elbows in order to make him back off."

Max laughed.

"Now, the maid of honor," she went on. "Elizabeth? Was that her name? Goodness, she certainly doesn't have her mother's sense of style."

"Well, let's see what she looks like tomorrow," I said.

"I doubt she'll do much better," Mom told me.

This was sort of a satisfaction. I still held Elizabeth to blame for making Debbie unhappy.

I wished I could give Debbie a magic amnesia pill. I wished I had an amnesia pill myself.

※※

After we had dropped Mom off and were heading back to my house, I slumped in the passenger seat like a sack of flour. "That was *work*," I told Max.

"Which part of it?" he asked.

"All of it! So many people, so many nice-to-meet-yous!"

But we always had this discussion. I don't think I'd ever come home from a social event without feeling drained and exhausted. Max, on the other hand... Max was oblivious. Really he was no more adept than I was, but he just muddled through anyhow.

Back when the two of us were married, we were notorious for leaving parties before anybody else. "Oops! There go the Baineses!" our host would cry, and one of the guests might say, dryly, "What a surprise." I kind of missed those days, I mean just in that one respect. It's hard to leave early when there's only one person doing it. So now when Max said, "I have to say, that mother of Kenneth's is a lot to deal with," I perked right up and said, "*Tell* me about it."

"Do you think she'll take over the marriage the way she's taking over the wedding?"

"Well, bear in mind—" I began.

Bear in mind that Debbie's no weakling, I was about to tell him. But then I rethought that. I wasn't so sure anymore, so I didn't finish my sentence. I merely shrugged.

We rode the rest of the way in silence. When we reached Ripken Street, Max pulled into the parking space behind my Corolla, once again closer than need be, and turned off the ignition but went on sitting there. I looked over at him. He was staring straight ahead. It was so quiet that I could hear the whiskery sound of his breathing. "Gail," he said finally, "when you said that Debbie had to trust Kenneth completely, she had to feel she could rely on every single word he said till the end of their days, did you mean that literally?"

"Of course," I said.

"You meant without a single lapse. Without the slightest slip-up. Zero mistakes allowed."

"We're talking about our very own daughter's marriage, Max," I said. "There's no off-and-on about it. No, 'Oh, well, whatever.'"

"Right," he said.

Then he let out an extra-long breath and said, "I realize I'm not going to win this one."

It was so typical. We'd be getting along just fine and then he'd say something that reminded me he was this totally other, totally opposite kind of person from me. I yanked my door open and got out of the car. I was halfway up the front steps before I heard him open his own door.

In the living room, a single lamp was glowing on a side table. I could barely make out the shapes of the furniture in the dimness, but I saw little white bits of something scattered across the rug, and more bits on the couch, and more leading off toward the kitchen. "What on earth," I said. I switched on the overhead light. The bits were paper, the translucent kind like toilet paper; and sure enough, next to the rug I saw a naked cardboard tube. "*Oh*, boy," Max said. He called, "Kitty-kitty?"

"Here she is," I said. She was curled up in the armchair she'd occupied before, wearing a frowsy, confused look as if we'd wakened her from a nap. I tut-tutted at her and she blinked, all innocence.

Max stooped to begin plucking the bits one by one from the rug, and I went to fetch the vacuum cleaner. "This is *not* what I would call being a good guest," he was telling the cat when I got back. I plugged in the vacuum cleaner and turned it on, and she grew more alert but she didn't run away. "I guess she felt we'd left her alone too long," Max told me.

"Evidently," I said. The vacuum cleaner was an upright, but I was able to heave it onto the couch to tackle the cushions. When I moved on to the chairs, the cat rose from hers in a leisurely fashion and dropped to the floor and left, tail high in the air.

"Was that really just one single roll?" Max asked. He had picked up the cardboard tube from the floor and was studying it. "How did she make such a mess?"

"I imagine it was quite a project," I told him.

Max went off to the kitchen to dispose of the tube, and I unplugged the vacuum cleaner and returned it to the coat closet.

When I came out to the kitchen, Max was standing in front of the fridge and surveying the contents. "Thinking of getting myself a beer," he told me. "How about you?"

"No, thanks."

I paused a moment.

"I was wondering if Debbie might call," I said finally.

"She won't call."

"Just to rehash the rehearsal, I mean."

"Not going to happen," he said.

He chose a can of Old Dundalk and closed the fridge door. You would think the man lived here.

"Well," I told him. "Maybe I'll head off to bed."

"What—now? It's barely nine o'clock!"

"It's been a long day. Feel free to stay up yourself, though."

"Oh. Okay. So, good night, I guess."

As I left the room, he was settling into the chair that reclined. He tipped it back as far as it would go and said, "Aah, me." It was half a yawn and half a sigh.

I climbed the stairs and went into my room, where I

switched a lamp on, closed the door—but then just plunked myself down on the edge of my bed and stared into space.

Max was right: she wasn't going to call. Why should she call? She had her own separate life now. She always had.

Eventually, I rose and got ready for bed. Then I slipped between the sheets and turned off the lamp. A pale, glowing arc swung across my ceiling from a passing car, and I heard faint music in the distance.

After a moment I threw my blanket aside so I was lying under just a sheet. I sat up again to puff my pillow and I lay back down.

A few minutes later my door made an unlatching sound, and the vertical line of light at its edge grew wider and the cat padded in. Her footsteps were clearly audible; that was how heavy she was. I felt her dent my mattress as she sprang onto it.

But here's what was weird: for one split second there, I'd thought it was Max at the door. I had felt this stab of outrage: Was there no escaping the man?

Anger feels so much better than sadness. Cleaner, somehow, and more definite. But then when the anger fades, the sadness comes right back again the same as ever.

two

D-DAY

Debbie did call, as it happened.

She called us on the morning of her wedding day. Called Max, to be specific. We were in the kitchen at the time. Max was flipping an omelet on the stove, and when his phone rang he pulled it from his pocket and glanced at the screen and told me, "Debbie," as he punched the screen. "Hello?" he said.

I set a bowl of kibble on the floor for the cat and went to stand next to him.

"Well, yes, I was; why do you ask?" he was saying into the phone. And then, "No, I didn't, because the only one I have is winter weight." He glanced over at me and mouthed, *"Suit."*

"What?" I said.

"She wants to know if I'm planning to wear last night's sports coat to the wedding. Or did I happen to bring a suit with me, she wonders."

"Uh-oh," I said.

Debbie said something else.

Max said, "That's very nice of you, hon. But you've got a big day ahead! How about I just ask your mom to give my sports coat a good ironing. I think that should do it."

I couldn't hear what she answered. I asked Max, "What's she saying?"

"She wants to come take us suit shopping," he told me.

"Oh!" I said. "Tell her we'll go."

"We will?" he asked.

"It'll be just the three of us!" I said, barely above a whisper. "Take her up on it. Say we'll do it."

"Your mom says we should say yes," he said into the phone. "Right. No, that's not necessary; I can—okay, see you then."

He put his phone back in his pocket. "She's coming by at a quarter of ten," he said. "We're going to hit Lerner Brothers the instant they open and buy something right off the rack and have her back home in time for the cosmetic person."

"What did you say was not necessary?" I asked him.

"That she should pay for it."

"No, certainly not," I said. "But don't you see? This is perfect! Even if it takes just an hour or two, we'll have one last chance to reason with her."

"Gail," he said. "No."

"I won't be pushy. I promise! I'll be very subtle. I won't tell her not to marry him; I'll just suggest she spend more time on her decision."

"What is *with* you, Gail? Why are you interfering in this?"

"For the same reason I'd interfere if I saw my two-year-old preparing to jump off a cliff," I told him.

"This is not a two-year-old, Gail. She's a fully grown woman, and she's choosing to marry somebody who made one single mistake."

"See? See there? You don't believe him either! You just admitted he did it!"

"I misspoke," he said. "You confused me."

"*That's* the part that gets me," I said. "That he wouldn't tell her the truth."

"No, it 'got' you, as you put it, before he'd told her a thing."

I hate the way Max pursues an argument into the ground. It used to wear me out, back when we were married. "Can we just drop this?" I said.

"You're the one who brought it up."

"Fine, I'll change the subject. How'd you sleep?" I asked him.

"I had this really embarrassing dream."

Oh, yes, another of Max's flaws was that he was fond of recounting his dreams, and they were always interminable. Now he said, as he served up my share of the omelet, "I dreamed I sent my principal a sympathy note but then I realized no one had died."

"Who did you *think* had died?" I asked.

"His wife. I had dropped my note in the corner mailbox, and so in order to get it back I made this sort of fishing-rod arrangement with a length of string and a wad of chewed gum..."

I sighed and took a bite of my omelet. It wasn't bad, actually.

"Then when that didn't work I thought, I know what! If he has one of those letter boxes on the outside of his house, I mean just hanging by his front door, I could wait behind a bush for his mailman to show up, and then..."

What with my worries about Debbie, I'd neglected to pursue the issue of my employment situation. Now I pondered my choices. Max had a point about those students who had a thing against math: I had always loved changing their minds. I waited for him to take a breath (he had reached one of those non sequitur moments that often occur in dreams, where he found himself all at once on a cruise ship), and then I said, "Do you suppose it takes a lot of red tape these days to get a teaching job?"

"Excuse me?" he said.

"I'd like to go back to teaching, but would that even be possible now? I'm not sure I have the proper certification anymore."

He studied me. "What *you* need," he said finally, "is a thunder jacket."

"A what?"

"One of those really snug jackets they put on dogs who are scared of thunder. I mean, good grief! Do you keep an itemized list of things to worry about? How do you remember them all?"

"But wouldn't this jacket have four sleeves?" I asked. "What'll I do with the extra two?"

"Add that to your worry list," he suggested.

I laughed and stood up to fetch the coffeepot.

"You want to come teach where I teach?" he asked.

I said, "You know I can't leave Baltimore. I've still got my mother here."

And besides, there was Debbie. But I didn't say that part.

"The head of *my* school is really nice," Max said. "He and his wife invite me over for all the major holidays."

"Maybe they're going to stop doing that, now that you've sent him your condolences," I said.

"No, it was my principal I sent condolences to. The principal and the head of my school are two different people."

I plugged the coffeepot back in and sat down. I said, "We need to decide what we're going to say to Debbie."

"*We're* not going to say anything to Debbie."

"I'm glad she's giving us this chance to talk to her," I said, "but I hate that it's because she suddenly cares what you're wearing. This is all on account of the Baileys, I tell you. Debbie never used to mind in the least what we wore! Now I'm wondering if it's the Baileys' doing that she offered to take me dress shopping. And the spa day, come to think of it. She's never been to a spa in her life!"

"She's never had a wedding in her life," Max pointed out.

"Do you suppose she's going over to *their* side?"

"What side is that?" he asked.

"Just . . . you know. Different from us."

He paused in the middle of raising his coffee cup. "That's the first time in a long, long while that you've said there was an 'us,'" he told me.

"Hmm? No, I just meant—I remember how I felt when I was young myself. I felt kind of ashamed of my parents. They didn't play golf or tennis or go to charity balls."

"*My* parents were very fond of them," Max said.

"I know that," I said. Then I said, "I'm the one your parents had trouble with. I wasn't huggy and touchy-feely enough."

"Now, now. They liked you very much," he said.

Notice he didn't say "loved."

Another thing that might have put them off was how he introduced me. He brought me to their house unannounced on our way to dinner one evening, and, "Mom!" he shouted. "Dad! Here's Gail! You finally get to meet Gail!" Lord knows how he'd advertised me beforehand. And I, of course, was so anxious about making a good impression that I closed up like some kind of turtle. I couldn't help it. I knew I was doing it, but I couldn't behave any differently.

If my parents approved of the marriage because Max thought I hung the moon, Max's parents probably did *not* approve for the very same reason. Their son had brought home this aloof, stiff girl who he claimed could do no wrong. He claimed he was the luckiest man in the world to have such a girl even notice him. I could see their side of it now. If not then.

And I can just about guarantee that if they had lived long enough to witness our divorce, they would have told Max, "No surprise to us!"

Debbie arrived exactly on time, at a quarter till ten. I was watching for her at the front window so she wouldn't have to park. "You sit up front," Max told me as we crossed the porch. I didn't argue. I wanted a closeup view of her; I needed to gauge her mood.

Her mood seemed fine, as far as I could tell. "Morning, you two!" she said as we climbed into her car. She was wearing jeans and a chambray shirt and not a bit of makeup, although her hair still hung to her shoulders. Generally, she put it in a ponytail on weekends. I guessed she didn't want to cause any crimp marks.

"Happy wedding day, hon," Max said from the backseat. "It's nice of you to start it off by taking your parents shopping."

"I'm just trying to fill the time," she told him. She checked her side mirror and then pulled out into the street. "Nothing's going to happen till two p.m., when Darleen comes to make us all up again."

"What's your lunch plan?" I asked. In Debbie's position, I couldn't have managed even a bite of lunch.

But she said, "Kenneth's mom is bringing sushi."

"Ah," I said. Then I said, "Will she be eating it with you?"

"Hmm? I don't know," she said, flicking her turn signal on. "I mean, maybe she will; I didn't ask."

She would, I could guarantee. Otherwise, why not just order by phone and have it delivered? She would bring the sushi to Debbie's door and make a halfhearted move to back out again but the girls would say, politely, "Oh, don't feel you need to go!" and she would say, "Well, just half a minute, maybe . . ."

"We might get some actual sunshine," Max announced. He spoke too quickly, too loudly; I bet he thought I was about to say something disparaging about Sophie. But I wouldn't have done that! I just smiled fiercely out my side window.

Debbie said, "I hope you're right."

I should have offered to bring lunch myself. I didn't know mothers could do that.

"Will you be staying out of the groom's sight today?" Max asked. "Or has that tradition changed?"

"I won't be laying eyes on him," Debbie said. "He doesn't even know what I'm going to be wearing. I just told him it would be street length, so he wouldn't think he needed a tux."

We passed my school, and I looked away because even though it was a Saturday, I worried someone might spot me. ("What can Gail Baines be up to, I wonder, lurking around the Ashton School? Everyone knows she lacks people skills.")

We passed the little soda shop where our students hung out after class, and the lake trout joint, and Mayella's Produce with its sidewalk display of fruits that always had a withered look. Debbie was telling us how Kenneth's grandmother had given them her entire chest of antique silverware. "A really beautiful pattern," she said, "with some pieces I don't even know the purpose of. Knives with these odd notches to them and forks with only two prongs."

"Good grief," I said. "How will you keep it all polished?"

"That's no problem. If you use silver every day it will stay polished on its own."

"You're going to use the oyster forks every day?"

"Is that what they are? Oh. Well..."

From the backseat, Max said, "Am I right in assuming that I can get an extra day's wear out of the shirt I wore last night?"

Debbie glanced at him in the rearview mirror. "You didn't bring another?" she asked.

"Not one with a collar."

She rolled her eyes at me.

"We'll find one at Lerner Brothers," I told her.

"This is getting expensive," Max said.

"I *told* you I'd like to pay for it," she said.

"No, no..."

I don't know why he'd mentioned the expense. Lerner Brothers was about as cut-rate as you could get.

And sure enough, when we walked through their front door, passing a rack of boxer shorts in three-packs and a counter piled high with track shoes, what should we find but a sign advertising ALL SUITS 40% OFF. "See there? It was meant to be," Max told us, just as if this trip had been entirely his idea. He and Debbie headed toward where the suits hung, while I made a side trip to a display of shirts. I knew his size, but I worried these might be skimpy, so I rummaged through them looking for a cut that could handle his barrel shape. And had he packed a tie? Just to be safe, I selected one from a counter of unwrapped ties all tangled together like castoffs. Navy blue with tiny white stars, I chose. That would go with just about anything.

By the time I reached the suit rack, Max had already disappeared into one of the changing booths and Debbie was sitting nearby in the shoe department, scrolling through her phone. "What do you think?" I asked, dropping into the chair beside her. I held up the tie, and she nodded. "As long as he doesn't decide on the brown," she told me. "He took a brown suit and a black and a navy into the booth with him."

"Brown!" I said. "I don't think so."

"Well, he didn't seem to feel strongly about any of them, so why don't we push the navy," she said.

"As long as it halfway fits," I told her. "It's not as if Lerner Brothers has its own tailor on the premises."

"Right."

She went back to her phone.

The sound system was playing "By the Time I Get to Phoenix." An elderly couple was chuckling together over by the T-shirts, the wife holding up one that was printed with some kind of caption.

"Debbie," I said. I cleared my throat.

"Hmm?" she said, not looking up.

"Deb, do you realize how permanent this is?"

Now she did look up. "Actually, it's not," she said. "As you should know better than anyone."

"But nobody *wants* a divorce," I told her. "No one goes into a marriage saying, 'Oh, well, I can always walk out tomorrow if I happen to change my mind.'"

"In fact, I imagine quite a few people do," she said. And she went back to her phone.

So I decided to let it go. It would kill me if my only daughter stopped speaking to me on her wedding day.

At that point, though, she abruptly dropped her phone into her purse and turned to face me. "Okay, Mom," she said. "You want to know what I think?"

I braced myself.

"I think that just because of your own experience, you're bound and determined that the man in the situation should have to face the music."

"*My* experience! What are you talking about?"

"I can put two and two together! I've never asked the particulars, and I'm not asking now. I honestly don't want to know. But I'll tell you this much: I have had a lifelong education in what *not* to do. I refuse to be one of those wives who hold a grudge forever. Who won't forgive their husbands for one little stupid mistake."

I said, "But—"

"How do I look?" Max asked.

He looked like a funeral director. Well, except for his crewnecked top. But the suit he wore over it was made of a hard, shiny material so intensely black that it turned his skin ashen. It made him seem dead, almost.

Right at that moment, though, I didn't feel able to tell him that. I couldn't make myself do it. His expression was so hopeful; he wore this hopeful, trusting smile. Clearly, he thought he looked wonderful.

It was Debbie who said, finally, "Try the navy."

His smile faded. "Really?" he asked. He looked over at me. "What do *you* think?" he asked me.

"Yes, maybe the . . . navy," I said faintly.

"Excuse me?"

"Try the navy."

"Oh," he said.

He looked down at one sleeve regretfully, and then he turned to go back to the changing booth.

"And put this shirt on underneath!" I called. I stood up, waving the shirt I'd chosen. "Put this tie on!"

"I've already got a tie," he said over his shoulder. "And I won't have to put any of it on, because the navy is the exact same style as the black."

I hadn't really paid close attention to the black, beyond the issue of its color. But I let it go. I returned the tie to its counter and sat down again next to Debbie. "Luckily," I told her, "no one actually looks at the father of the bride."

"Right," she said. She was studying her phone again. She said, "Guess what: Bitsy has hives."

"Hives!"

"She thinks it's something she ate last night."

"What a pity," I said. "Deb—"

"Maybe the pineapple in the chicken dish, she thinks."

I forced myself to consider the subject at hand. I said, "Can she still be in the wedding?"

"She can still be in the wedding, but her face will scare small children, she says."

"Well, no one looks at the bridesmaids, either," I told her.

This made her laugh. She said, "Now, there you might be stretching things, Mom."

"I'm right, though," I said. "Aren't I right?" I asked Max,

because he was walking toward us now, wearing his everyday clothes again and clutching the navy suit in a bunch under one arm. "Nobody looks at anyone but the bride, when they go to weddings."

"Absolutely," he said, and he dropped the suit on top of the shirt in my lap. "Which is why my khaki sports coat would have been fine; believe me."

Debbie returned her phone to her purse and stood up. "Bitsy's got hives," she told him as we walked toward the checkout counter. "She thinks it was last night's pineapple."

"Right, in the chicken dish," Max said.

I said, "You had the chicken dish too?"

"I did."

"I thought you were vegetarian!"

"I am, but I've never really felt that chickens were sentient beings."

I sent Debbie a resigned look, but I don't think she caught it.

Once we had paid for our purchases—once Max had paid—and we were out on the street again, Debbie said, "There! That's done. Time to get home before my bridesmaids arrive."

"Thanks again, hon," Max told her. "I appreciate your helping out like this."

Which I had to admit was gracious of him, since it was only for her sake that he had agreed to the trip.

The rain was still holding off, although the air felt damp and heavy. I hoped it wasn't going to turn hot; Debbie's wedding dress had a high neckline. But maybe she wouldn't notice the heat. Maybe she would be one of those brides so buoyant with happiness, so positively airborne, that the weather wouldn't cross her mind.

To me, though, she didn't seem that way. She seemed like our regular low-key Debbie, steering capably through the Saturday-morning traffic. Although I was sitting in back this time, since I had somehow ended up with the bulky Lerner Brothers bag, and I couldn't see her expression.

All three of us rolled our windows down, and Debbie turned her radio on. They were delivering the sports news. The Orioles were doing well, it seemed, and Debbie was of the opinion that they just might keep it up. Max said he agreed. "I really think they might make it to the World Series this year," he told her.

I happened to know that Max couldn't care less about the World Series. He was only trying to connect with his beloved daughter. And something about this, coupled with my memory of his trusting smile as he'd stood posing in that ghastly black suit, hurt my heart. I can't put it any other way. It hurt my heart.

We pulled up in front of my house, and he leaned over to give Debbie a peck on the cheek before he got out. But I had that bag to maneuver, so I was just shutting the car door behind me while he was already climbing the steps to the porch. I paused next to Debbie's window and said, "Deb—"

And she said, "Mom—"

She was afraid I was going to raise the subject of Kenneth again, I could tell. She wanted to forestall me. But I overrode whatever she was about to say. I said, "Deb, I can't let you go on thinking . . . I know what you're thinking. But that's not fair to your dad. It wasn't your dad. It was me."

She said, "What?"

"It was me who made the stupid mistake," I said.

She opened her mouth and drew in a breath to speak, but then she just sat looking at me, both hands gripping the steering wheel.

I couldn't bear it anymore. I walked away.

⁕

This time when we entered the house we found everything as we'd left it, which I took to mean the cat was feeling more comfortable. Not that I wanted her to get *too* comfortable, of course. She strolled down the stairs to greet us with a mild "meow" and then continued into the kitchen, where I heard the rattle of kibble a moment later.

"You want me to model my new suit?" Max asked.

"I'll just wait till the wedding," I told him.

Because his suit was the last thing on my mind right now, in fact. I was thinking about what I'd said to Debbie. I was experiencing this out-of-breath sensation, as if I'd just done something dangerous, and I had to collect myself before I spoke again. "It's not as if we could do anything about it at this late date," I told him.

"Actually," Max said, "we could do a *little* something."

I gave him a wary look.

He said, "You could maybe shorten the sleeves a tad."

"Uh-oh."

"Just a tiny amount, I promise. Just an inch or two."

"An inch or two!" I said. "Honestly, Max."

But I handed him the Lerner Brothers bag, and he dumped it onto the couch and took out the coat and shrugged himself into it. He was right: the sleeves extended all the way to his knuckles. "Why didn't you just try on another size?" I asked him.

"I didn't want to use up any more of Debbie's time," he said.

"Instead you're going to use up *my* time."

"Yes, but you have more of it," he pointed out.

Well, I couldn't argue with that. I had all the time in the world, sad to say. I went to fetch my sewing box.

While I was pinning the sleeves up—Max standing in front of me with both arms stiffly straight, like an obedient child—he said, "I was thinking that after this, I could invite you out to lunch."

"That's okay," I said. "Thanks anyhow."

"I could take you to the Cultured Crab; how about it?"

"We've got plenty of food here," I told him.

"Like what?"

"Like these frozen chicken pot pies that are really delicious, since I know now that you eat chicken. All they need is microwaving."

"Wouldn't you rather have a crab dish?"

"I'm actually not all that hungry," I said. I stripped the suit coat off of him, careful of the pins, and started digging through the sewing box for navy thread.

"Well, of course you're not," he said after a moment. "I don't know what I was thinking. This is kind of a fraught day for you."

"Yes, it is, kind of," I said.

Because I wasn't about to admit that I just didn't want to leave the house for fear I'd miss a phone call from Debbie.

Maybe she would call as soon as she got home. She would

call my landline, knowing that my cell phone stayed in my purse, as a rule, and she would say . . . what? What was I hoping she would say?

I should have gone on standing next to her car window after I had confessed. I should have waited to hear her reaction. It was only that I'd been so terrified of what that reaction might be.

But in any case, she wasn't going to call. By now, she would have been home for some time. She could easily have called if she had wanted to.

Still, I chose the chair closest to the phone when I sat down to thread my needle.

"We'll just stay here and have comfort food," Max was saying. "Cozy little chicken pot pies! I can do the microwaving."

"Thank you, Max," I said. I really meant it. I looked up from my sewing and said, "Thank you very much."

So he went off to the kitchen.

I snipped the thread on the first sleeve and went on to the other.

Max, now: that much I could console myself with. At least I had cleared his name with her, even though he would never realize it.

I envisioned him as he had looked in his dead-black suit, so hopeful and so unaware, the kind of man who would never, ever in his life knowingly harm another person, and my mood lifted, gradually. My breathing grew even again. I sewed dots of tiny navy-blue stitches, and with each stitch I felt calmer.

Even when he asked after lunch if I happened to know what to do in case a little pot pie goo had somehow stuck itself to the floor of the microwave, I just shrugged and told him not to worry about it.

While Max was taking his afternoon nap, I ironed his sleeves flat. Then I touched up my own dress, just to keep myself busy, and I tracked down a manila envelope for the photo display. For a moment I considered making a run to the reception site to arrange the photos ahead of time, but that seemed sort of silly since there were only six of them. Instead, I sat down on the living room couch and petted the cat for a while. She allowed it, more or less. She stirred and said, "Mmph," but went on sleeping.

I wondered if Sophie were still at Debbie's house, chitchatting with the girls and eating sushi. No, by now she must be home again, maybe dressing for the wedding. I was curious about what she'd wear. Part of me hoped she was one of those mothers-in-law who tried to upstage the bride—wore something fancier than the bride's dress, maybe even something off-white. But I knew that was ridiculous. Sophie had more common sense than that. I was just feeling jealous because I worried Debbie might start preferring her to me.

When Debbie was a little girl, way before Max and I divorced, she'd had a habit of falling in love with other people's families. She would come home from her friends' houses wishing that we too lived out in the country and staged giant family reunions and holiday celebrations. Why, oh, why was she an only child? she wanted to know. I explained that we couldn't afford more children—not if she wanted the very best college education. "See there?" she said. "You're always trying to do things perfect, when I'd rather do things just so-so but have lots of brothers and sisters."

"Perfect*ly*," I corrected her.

I didn't let on that I'd been fielding such complaints for most of my life. Couldn't I ever settle for just *okay*? I'd been asked more than once.

<hr />

At three thirty I climbed the stairs with our two outfits draped over my arm. I stopped outside the guest room to knock, thinking Max might need to be wakened, but he opened the door immediately and said, "Hi."

"We should be leaving in half an hour," I said as I handed over his suit. "Remember we have to pick up my mother."

"I remember."

I went on to my own room and laid my dress across the bed. It still felt a little bit warm from the iron. Maybe I would just skip the pantyhose, I decided. My skirt reached to mid-calf, after all.

In my bathroom mirror, I looked old. People don't warn you ahead of time that some days your face will be netted with wrinkles and other days almost smooth. Today I was wrinkly. My eyes were quirked into triangles and so many lines crossed my forehead that it resembled a sheet of ruled paper. But at least my hair hung vertically. No trace anymore of the beauty parlor experiment.

I dressed without checking the mirror again and went back downstairs. Max arrived a moment later, wearing his new suit and shirt and a really ugly tie, royal blue slashed with yellow lightning bolts. He was still in his everyday shoes, though—black canvas with crepe soles. Well, nothing to be done about that now. At least he wasn't looking old.

Although who could tell, under that stubble? Men had all the advantages.

The rain was still holding off, for the moment, and people were going ahead with their usual Saturday plans. Family cars drove past with beach chairs piled on their roof racks, and station wagons were double-parked to pick up swarms of children lugging sports equipment. I started worrying we'd be late. Then when we reached Mom's apartment building we saw no sign of her, although usually she'd be waiting out front. "Of all times," I said, and I took out my phone and punched her number.

"Hello?" she asked finally, in a tone so tentative that you'd never guess she had caller ID.

"Where *are* you, Mom?" I asked. "We're down here waiting."

"Well, I could have been there by now if my phone hadn't started ringing."

I rolled my eyes at Max. "We're sitting in front of your building," I said, "parked in a no-parking zone." I hung up and put my phone away. "I mean, the woman's up before dawn seven days a week," I told Max. "Why does she choose today of all days to dawdle?"

"Aw, now," he said. "Cut her a little slack, Gaily-girl."

"Could you *please* not call me Gaily-girl?"

"My apologies, madam."

I folded my arms across my chest and glared out the windshield, and Max shut off his engine. When I heard my mother fumbling at the rear door I didn't even turn my head.

"*So* sorry!" Mom caroled as she got in.

"We're in no hurry," Max assured her.

"Speak for yourself," I told him. He restarted the car and pulled out into traffic, while I twisted around in my seat to inspect my mother's outfit. She was the only woman I knew who still wore a hat on special occasions. This one was narrow-brimmed and tilted, with a ruche of white chiffon poking up at one side like a handful of Kleenex.

"I suppose I could have caught a ride with a friend," she was saying, "except they've all turned into such bad drivers lately. I would hate to end up dead on my only granddaughter's wedding day."

"Oh, we just wouldn't have told her till after the ceremony," I said in a soothing voice.

Max gave a bark of laughter, but my mother said primly, "That would probably have been wisest," and turned to look back at a young girl waiting on the curb in what had to be last night's outfit—a transparent blue gauze sheath with a front slit rising all the way to her crotch. "Goodness," Mom murmured. "What kind of *underwear* would you need?"

Max said, "We did get a glimpse of Debbie this morning, incidentally. Looking very put together and self-possessed."

"Of course," my mother said. "She takes after me."

I wondered why it was that I had so many irritating people in my life.

Today the church parking lot was busier. I saw Max's niece Rose walking across the tarmac with her husband, and a trio of brightly dressed young women whom I didn't know, and Debbie's old piano teacher. Max chose a space next to Dave's convertible to pull into.

"Will this be a very *big* wedding?" my mother asked as she got out of the car.

"It's not supposed to be," I said, "but I do think Kenneth's parents have squeezed in a few extra guests."

In fact, they'd had a lot more to say about the arrangements than the groom's parents usually did, because they were footing most of the bills. Certainly Max and I couldn't have swung it. We'd been aiming for something lower-key; even Debbie and Kenneth had. But one thing led to another, as they say. The reception, for instance, would be taking place at a club that the Baileys belonged to, so they were the ones paying for that. I didn't even want to know how much it was costing them.

Our instructions were that we should wait with the bridal party in a small side room off the foyer until it was time for us to be seated, but first we had to connect my mother with an usher. It turned out to be the usher whose name I didn't know. He gave her a courtly bow before he offered her his arm, and she sailed away with her ruche bobbing jauntily on her hat brim.

In the side room we found the three bridesmaids gathered around Debbie, fussing with her dress in a way that struck me as needless. She already looked like a model on a magazine cover. In fact, I felt almost shy in her presence, and it wasn't only because of our most recent conversation. The dress was a deep emerald that brought out the gold in her hair, and her shoes were emerald too—ballerina flats because she hated heels. She had told her attendants they could wear whatever they liked as long as it was some shade of green, and Bitsy had chosen kelly green while Caroline was in a paler green flecked with white daisies, and Elizabeth wore an olive scoopneck. (The olive didn't really go with the other greens, in my opinion, but never mind.)

Max was the first to speak. "Oh, honey-bunny," was what he said, and his voice had a little break in it that made me instantly resolve to behave sensibly. I just said, "You look very nice, Deb," which didn't begin to convey how I *really* felt she looked.

"Thanks," she said. "Would you believe the flowers haven't come? We ordered them from Cindy Ross; you remember Cindy; she dropped out of college junior year to start her own florist shop and here I made such a big deal of ordering our flowers from her and she was supposed to bring them to the house in person while we were getting ready but *oh*, no, *oh*, no—"

"Never mind," Max assured her. "No one will notice they're missing. And look at you, Bitsy! Not a single hive! Or"—to himself—"would the singular be *hife*, I wonder."

He was being tactful, because she did have kind of a bumpy complexion. But she said, "You should have seen me when I first woke up! My mom said, 'Bitsy Taylor! You are surely not going to a wedding like that!'"

I felt a tap on my shoulder. "It's time," Dave told me.

I wanted to spend a few more moments with Debbie. I wanted to say . . . *I* don't know what. But I took Dave's arm and walked out of the room without another glance at her, and Max followed close behind.

The church was even fuller than I had expected. Most of the guests were on the groom's side, of course, but our own side was fairly well populated. As we proceeded up the center aisle I noticed Aunt Tess and her daughter Cheryl, and Debbie's tennis partner, and two of Debbie's friends from our carpool days along with, I guessed, their husbands. Up front in the lefthand aisle a lurking, shadowy figure startled me till I realized it was Spofford Talbot, Debbie's old high school classmate—an awkward, fumbling boy (*still* a boy) who was trying to make it as a freelance photographer. Sophie had wanted to bring in a team of professionals but Debbie had prevailed, and there he was, doing his best to shrink into the woodwork while tentatively snapping pictures. And all the while the organ was playing something murmury and generic, nattering away with no one listening.

Dave led me to the front pew and waited for me to sit down beside my mother. She gave me a brilliant fake smile and turned to face forward again. Then Max settled next to me. He sat with his back not quite touching the back of the pew, as if he were planning to jump up again at any moment.

The organ stopped, briefly, before it uttered a single crashing chord and swung into something purposeful. It wasn't "Here Comes the Bride" but something else; I couldn't say what. Something with almost a trumpet sound to it.

Reverend Gregory was waiting up front, dressed now in a sharply cut gray suit, and Kenneth and Jared stood beside him. To me Kenneth seemed his usual self, not noticeably tense or nervous. He wore a white carnation in his buttonhole, which surprised me. I had thought the bride's florist supplied the groom's flowers as well, but evidently not.

I don't know why I was focusing on the flower issue. I should have been watching for the bridal procession. Instead, I faced stubbornly forward and let everyone arrive unexpectedly—first Bitsy with the nameless usher, then Caroline with Dave, then Elizabeth on her own, carrying . . . oh! Carrying a bouquet. Something white and lacy. And the others carried flowers too, I realized belatedly, and so did Debbie, as I saw when she finally appeared. Her florist friend must have come through at the very last possible moment.

Debbie was the only one who walked normally, no little hitch in her step to acknowledge the music. And her expression was so serene, I was finally convinced that she must know what she was doing. She arrived at the front of the church; she handed her flowers to Elizabeth; she took her place next to Kenneth. He was smiling at her broadly, his whole face alight.

The organ fell silent. Reverend Gregory looked out at the congregation. "Dearly beloved," he began.

I kept my eyes very wide and tried to think non-teary thoughts. I made myself remember, for instance, how annoying Debbie had been when she was in her teens. She used to parrot these ridiculous phrases she must have picked up from her friends. "Youey tooey?" she would say, meaning "You too?" anytime she agreed with someone. It wasn't even natural-sounding! It had so clearly been invented! Recalling that phrase did me a lot of good. I began trying to think of some others.

"Who is it who blesses this couple's choice?" Reverend Gregory asked out of the blue. Or to *me* it seemed out of the blue. Max and I stood up together. Somehow Max already had hold of my hand, and now he squeezed my fingers and both of us said, "We do," in perfect unison.

Then things moved on. I don't recall Debbie and Kenneth saying their "I do"s, but of course they must have, and next thing I knew they were kissing. At that moment I remembered another of Debbie's phrases—this one from early childhood. She had fallen off a seesaw at nursery school and cut her forehead, and when she looked at her stitches later in the bathroom mirror she had asked, "Will I have permage?"

"Will you have *what*?" I asked.

"Will it stay this way always?"

"Oh! You mean 'permanent damage,' " I said.

"Will I, do you think?"

But that phrase, of course, had not annoyed me in the least. That phrase had merely amused me. "You're going to be good as new," I had told her.

And she was.

Kenneth took a step back and smiled down at her gravely, and then he tucked her hand in his arm and turned to lead her back up the aisle. The organist broke into Mendelssohn's "Wedding March"—following Reverend Gregory's playlist, finally—which seemed exactly right, because what could have sounded more joyous? The two of them very nearly skipped to the beat as they walked out.

There was a considerable period of milling and mixing among the guests after that. Of course they had to greet the people they knew, and introduce those people to other people, and talk amongst themselves. Kenneth's parents came over to tell us what a lovely bride Debbie made (Sophie in a perfectly appropriate mother-of-the-groom dress, needless to say), and I told them that Kenneth had looked very handsome. And we did say hello to Max's niece, and compliment Reverend Gregory on his ceremony, and give a wave to Spofford Talbot, although he was too busy fumbling with his camera to manage a real conversation. Out in the foyer a small crowd was gathering now around the bridal couple, but it wasn't my kind of scene, to be honest, or Max's either, and so eventually we looked at each other and I said, "Well? Should we be heading to the reception?"

"If you're sure it's not too soon," Max said, sending an edgy look toward the others.

"*Someone* has to be first," I told him. "Besides, I promised Sophie I would put those photos up."

We detoured to collect my mother from a group of her relatives, but she said she would hitch a ride with Aunt Tess. (Apparently she felt freer to die now that Debbie was married.) So Max and I left on our own, not talking. It was bliss not to talk. Although once we'd settled in the car and rolled our windows down, Max did say, "Well, then," on a long sigh. Then he sat for a moment with his hands at the base of the steering wheel before he started the engine.

The Clarion Club was way downtown, in that area I still thought of as new—that collection of luxury hotels and high-end restaurants and waterfront promenades where glamorous couples strolled by in their yachting clothes. To get to the club itself, we had to park in an underground lot and take an eerily silent, room-size elevator to the very top floor of a very tall building. There we found ourselves surrounded by massive plate-glass windows overlooking a harbor so distant and postcard perfect that a person had to ask, "This is . . . *what* city did you say this was?"

I had been there once before, at an auction dinner for the Ashton School, so I wasn't as dumbstruck as Max was. He stopped in his tracks the moment he stepped off the elevator, while I went directly to the front desk facing us. The maître d' stationed there said, "Ma'am?"

I said, "I'm just looking for—" but then I spotted the bulletin board next to him. "Oh, good," I said, and I drew the envelope of photos from my purse. Sophie had already put her own photos up, I saw. They were strung across the board with wide empty spaces between them: a baby boy laughing in a stroller, a toddler boy astride a plastic motorcycle, a grade-school boy in a Cub Scout uniform . . .

At the very bottom, all alone, centered very precisely, was an 8½ x 11 of Debbie and Kenneth together, finally—all grown up and arm in arm and dressed for some formal occasion, Debbie in a full-length gown and Kenneth in a tux.

I shook my photos out of the envelope and started tacking them up as Sophie had instructed—Debbie's baby photo in the space next to Kenneth's baby photo, her toddler photo in the space next to Kenneth's toddler photo, and so on. But if this project had been left up to me, I would have arranged a solid block of Debbie photos and then a solid block of Kenneth photos—or Kenneth photos and then Debbie photos; what did I care?—above the photo of the two of them. Because isn't that how it works, for most couples? You don't start out with someone next to you; you start out all alone. You go through infancy and childhood and adolescence, as a rule, before you meet your other person.

When I was finished, I stepped back to survey the final effect. "What do you think?" I asked Max. He was standing at my elbow with his head cocked. "I love the shoes," he told me. He meant the shoes that Debbie wore on the day she started first grade: saddle oxfords so new, so gigantic and so dazzlingly white, that she hadn't been able to take her eyes off them. All the observer saw of her was the top of her bent head.

The two of us stood staring at that photo for quite a while. You'd think there was no more fascinating sight than the center part, just the tiniest bit crooked, that separated Debbie's two heartbreaking pigtails.

Not counting the staff—the maître d', the barman at the drinks counter, and the DJ tinkering with his lineup of equipment—Max and I were the only ones there; so we had a little time to walk around casing the joint, as Max put it. All the tables were rectangular, draped in heavy white linen and set with gold-rimmed china and crystal stemware. The two at the front bore place cards, although elsewhere it appeared that people could settle wherever they chose. I had no hope of sitting at one of those myself, unfortunately. Max and I had been assigned to Table Two, along with Kenneth's parents and the two surviving grandmothers and Reverend and Mrs. Gregory. Table One was the bridal couple with their attendants and—I was guessing, here—the attendants' significant others. I wondered if Elizabeth had a significant other, but I couldn't tell from the place cards.

Once we'd made our circuit of the room, we returned to the area nearest the elevator where the guests were beginning to collect. A man in a sky-blue leisure suit was introducing himself to a woman with long white hair, and an ancient-looking couple was talking with another ancient-looking couple, and Spofford Talbot was trying to do something to his camera. "Get any good ones yet, Spofford?" I asked, because at least he was someone whose name I knew. But this rattled him so that he said, "Um . . ." and forgot to answer, so I took pity on him and backed off.

"Looks like I'll be joining you at the old folks' table," someone behind me said. I turned to find Jared. He was holding up two place cards as if they were winning lottery tickets.

I said, "Table One has an age limit?"

"No, but the groom is refusing to sit at the same table as his sister," Jared said. "Sibling rivalry makes no allowance for weddings, it turns out."

This was interesting. I said, "So . . . he's including *you* in that rivalry?"

"Not specifically," Jared said, "but since I'm the best man, I figure I ought to sit wherever the maid of honor sits." And he headed off toward Table Two with his place cards.

I looked around for Max, planning to fill him in on this latest development, but he was deep in conversation now with Spofford. Apparently he was having more success than I had had.

All this time, music had been playing in the background. Oldies, mostly: Joni Mitchell and Judy Collins and such. But the music came to a stop, all at once, and somehow people knew that they should turn to face the elevator. Debbie and Kenneth were just emerging from it, hand in hand. Then Anne Murray started singing "Could I Have This Dance?" and Kenneth took Debbie in his arms and twirled her around. Both of them wore somber expressions—frowns, almost—because, as I happened to know, neither was much of a dancer. But they did their best, and gradually they loosened up and Debbie even leaned back a bit to smile into Kenneth's eyes.

Could I have this dance, for the rest of my life? What a cataclysmic question, when you stopped to think about it. I wondered how it was that anyone on earth ever found the courage to marry.

But no one else seemed to wonder. The guests formed a circle around the couple, and when the dance was finished they clapped. Then after the briefest pause, the music swung into "Lean on Me," and Debbie turned and walked over to Max and held out her hand. Poor Max couldn't dance to save his soul, but he swallowed hard and squared his shoulders and gamely set a palm on her hip.

Debbie was the one who had selected that song, I supposed. Of course she was. And it did seem appropriate. (She and Max had always had a special connection. You had only to see how she gazed up at him now to know that.) After a few beats Kenneth stepped onto the floor with his mother, and I had a moment of panic when I wondered if I would have to dance with his father. But no, when the song was finished Debbie turned from Max to call out, "Come on, you guys!" and another song began—"Today," with the New Christy Minstrels—and Kenneth reclaimed Debbie while a dozen or so other young couples joined them. (I thought Kenneth's father looked as relieved as I felt.) When Max came back to stand next to me, I said, "Shall we get ourselves a drink?" and he said, "Yes!" like a man in a desert.

The bar was already surrounded by other dance-averse people, so I waited with Mom and my cousin Cheryl while Max threaded his way to the front of the line. Cheryl wanted to know how Debbie and Kenneth had met. "They went to law school together," I told her. "It wasn't love at first sight, though, or anything like that. More like a growing friendship, at least on Debbie's part."

"On Kenneth's part, though . . . ," Cheryl suggested with a glint of a smile.

"On Kenneth's part, I don't know," I said.

"Of course it was first sight for *him*!" my mother said. "Our Debbie? Our gorgeous Debbie? How could he resist her? Just from watching his face while they were dancing, you could tell he was totally smitten."

"That was concentration," I told her.

"Was what?"

"Concentration on getting the dance right."

"Honestly, Gail," my mother said, and she gave a dismissive snort and told Cheryl, "Gail doesn't have a romantic bone in her body, I swear. Her very own, darling own daughter, and yet she won't admit a young man could fall madly in love with her!"

"What can I say," I told her.

Because one of life's frustrations is that sometimes, it's best to say nothing.

When dinner was finally announced, I saw from the place cards on our table that Jared had created a space for himself at my left and for Elizabeth at her father's right. The new settings had clearly been arranged by an amateur, with the silverware slightly crooked and the bread plates on the wrong side. As I was assessing all this, Jared arrived next to me and pulled my chair out for me. "I figured you might actually welcome the extra company," he said in an undertone once I was seated. "It's awkward to be thrown together with an estranged spouse, don't you find?"

"Well, but——" I began.

But Max and I were not *estranged*, exactly, I wanted to say. Not after all this time. I stopped myself, though. No point going into it. And anyway, by now Max had taken his place on my right and was introducing me to the minister's wife, who sat at his other side. "How do you do," she said to me. "I am Marie-Louise." She had a very strong accent of some sort, and that announcing tone of voice that you often hear with certain foreigners. But she was extremely attractive—a stylish woman in her late forties, with dark hair that was cut way longer in front than in back.

"I guess you have to attend a lot of these things," Max told her.

"I do not," she said flatly. "But the Baileys are especial friends of ours, and supporters of our church."

I decided against telling her that *especial* was almost not used anymore.

The waiters were whisking our empty plates away and substituting filled plates. I had the salmon, and Max, it turned out, had ordered the prime rib. (I didn't say a word.) Jared and Elizabeth caused a small rush of confusion till their own choices were redirected to our table—prime rib for both of them. I was curious about Elizabeth's reaction to being banished from the bride and groom's table, but evidently she had taken that in stride. She was rolling her eyes now at her mother's comment on the centerpiece. ("Skimpy" was Sophie's verdict.)

Jared asked, close to my ear, "Are you still teaching, these days?"

I redirected my thoughts. I said, "Not exactly. I'm assistant headmistress at the Ashton School."

"Ah," he said. Then he gave me a long, searching look. "And are you happy in the life you've chosen, Gail?"

"Am I . . . ? Of course I'm happy," I said. Then I changed the subject. "I've been wondering why it is that you're Kenneth's best man. I've heard of the father being best man, but not, so far as I know, the uncle."

"Oh, Kenneth has always looked up to me," Jared said. "In fact, I took him hiking in Europe the summer after his high school graduation and we got along like a house afire, really better than he and his father ever did, I have to say . . ."

And he was off and running, telling how he himself was a very experienced hiker, unlike Kenneth's father, who was more of a couch potato; how even with the age difference Kenneth had trouble keeping up with him when they climbed Mount—

Till Sophie lowered the index card she'd been studying and gave him a look. "Pay attention, please, Jared," she said. "You're going to offer a toast to Debbie."

"I am?" he asked.

"'Best man toasts the bride,'" she said, reading from her card. "Immediately after the cake is served. You stand up and propose a toast."

"Got it," he said.

"I can offer you some pointers if you're wondering what to—"

"I've got it, Sophie."

"Then the maid of honor toasts the groom," she told Elizabeth. "That would be you, dear."

Elizabeth was discussing some sort of transportation issue with her grandmother, but her response was instantaneous. "No," she said. She didn't so much as turn her head. She told her grandmother, "I can give Aunt Bee a ride too, if she needs one."

"What do you mean, 'no'?" Sophie asked.

Now Elizabeth did turn. She said, "Why would I toast somebody who doesn't even want me sitting at his table?"

"But he's your brother!" Sophie said. "I don't care *what* silly spat you're having!"

Max, of all people, was the one who saved the day. He asked Sophie, "Who comes next?"

"Pardon?"

"Who offers the next toast after the maid of honor?"

"Why, the host," Sophie said.

"The host?"

"'The host of the reception, which is to say the father of the bride and/or the financer of the reception,'" she read off from her card.

"So let's jump ahead to the host," Max told her. "Meaning me."

It could also mean Rupert, but Sophie was nice enough not to point that out. She sent Elizabeth a frown, and then she said, "Well, I suppose that's how we'll have to do it. So first you'd toast Debbie and Kenneth, Max, and then you would welcome the guests."

"Consider it done," Max said, and he picked up his fork.

Sophie couldn't resist one last glare at Elizabeth, but Elizabeth was absorbed now in her grandmother's description of totaling her Oldsmobile. Or she *seemed* absorbed, at least. Although she had that ears-perked posture of someone listening to a whole other conversation elsewhere.

My salmon was like a shoe sole, no surprise. Everyone said the prime rib was excellent, though. By now the talk was general. The grandmother widened her discussion of her car wreck to include the entire table, and Rupert chimed in with a wreck *he* had had, a couple of years ago. True to form, he insisted on supplying every last eentsy detail. "This was right around Christmastime," he said. "Or no, I'm lying to you; it was more like New Year's. I remember distinctly, because . . ." For once, I didn't feel the least bit impatient. I was just happy no one was counting on me to help fill the airwaves.

But then: "I have to say," Jared said, close to my ear. "It was a real surprise when you took up with Max Baines."

I turned. I said, "Um——"

"Usually a person would announce such things to someone she was currently dating, but I just had to draw my own conclusions when I saw you out and about with him."

"Well, he was a friend!" I said.

Jared drew back and gazed at me meaningfully, as if I had proved his point.

Anyhow. I turned back to the others. People were eating their salads now; we had finished the main course. Salad at the end of the meal: that always struck me as foreign. Maybe it was Marie-Louise's influence, if she and the Baileys were so chummy.

In fact, a cross-cultural issue seemed to be the subject of the current conversation. Marie-Louise, who had just waved away the offering of a second dinner roll, asked seemingly out of the blue if Americans used the word 'fool' in polite society. Everyone looked puzzled, but Max said, "I do remember that we weren't allowed to say *fool* in front of my great-aunt. She was a foot-washing Baptist, and she claimed there's a passage in the Bible that expressly forbids it."

"Ah," Marie-Louise said. "Thank you for straightening this out. We were always told as children that after a large meal we should never say we were fool."

The others fell silent, briefly. Then my mother asked, "Because you were . . . fool of food?"

"Yes."

A soft "Oh!" traveled around the table.

"In my country," Marie-Louise said, "the word has a sexual connotation."

Max said, "A . . . ?"

"It has to do with the engorged male member, you understand."

"Okay," Max said. "Well, just to back up for a moment, here—"

"Or maybe drop it altogether!" Reverend Gregory said in a bright tone of voice.

"Yes, of course, we shall drop it," Marie-Louise said hastily, and we all got very busy with our salads.

After the salad came the wedding cake, finally. Seven towering layers topped with a heap of sugar roses, riding on a wheeled cart propelled by two very focused waiters. Everybody oohed and aahed, and Sophie said, sternly, "I trust you all saved room!"

Max told me, under his breath, "Trust you're not too—"

I gave him a sideways kick beneath the table, and then both of us sat straighter and faced forward.

There was some confusion about the toasts. First, the timing. Sophie had said the toasts should take place immediately after the cake was served, but *how* immediately? Did that mean even before people had picked up their forks? But how would they know to wait? So maybe it meant while they were actually eating. No, that seemed just plain wrong, to have the scraping of plates and the munching sounds drowning out the toasts. Surely it made more sense to get the eating over with first.

It was Sophie herself debating this now, with some input from her mother-in-law and from Rupert, but it was Jared who pointed out the scraping-of-plates factor, and that settled it. We went ahead and dug into our cake. (At some of the tables, people had already started.) This was a lemon-flavored cake, with grated lemon rind in the frosting—better than your average wedding cake. And the waiters came around with coffee and tea, and we were finishing our cake and beginning to relax and nod passively as Rupert launched into a description of his and Sophie's own wedding cake, a portion of which they'd hand-fed to each other according to the custom, although they hadn't done that crazy thing of smushing it into each other's face... when Sophie said, severely, "Now your toast, please, Jared," and Jared said, "Yes, *ma'am*," and pushed his chair back and stood up and tinkled his knife against his champagne glass. Table by table, the others stopped talking, and Jared turned to the head table, where Kenneth and Debbie sat watching him expectantly. "I would like to offer a toast to Deborah, our beautiful bride," he said. "The only woman I know of who could make Kenneth pass up his poker night for a lecture on the legal rights of undocumented immigrants."

Here and there people chuckled, and Debbie smiled and mouthed a silent "Thank you" to Jared. Then he went on to welcome her to the family, and to make a little crack about how she'd have to learn to put up with Rupert's dad jokes, after which he raised his glass and took a sip from it and sat back down. I felt Max beginning to collect himself next to me, but before he could stand up there was a sudden shriek of chair legs on the other side of the table and Elizabeth stood instead, already holding her glass high. "And *I* propose a toast to the groom," she said. "Here's to you, Kenneth, my very dear brother—for the most part." More chuckles, all from tables other than our own. (Our own was more alert to the possibility of pitfalls.) "We've had some good times together," Elizabeth told Kenneth, "including several when you totally saved my ass, and I wish you many more good times with your darling Debbie." And she tipped her glass toward the couple and then took a sip.

Kenneth said, "Thank you, sis." Then he said. "I mean it. Thanks," and I don't think I was imagining things when I say there was a certain misty look to his eyes.

Some of the people who were in the know—Elizabeth's father, her grandmother, Jared—made soft sounds of approval as Elizabeth sat back down, and Sophie said, "That was very sweet, dear," and gave her an approving smile.

After that, things came to a stop, for a moment. Then Sophie said, "Max?" and Max said, "Huh?"

"Your toast?"

"Oh," he said.

This time, he made it to a standing position. "Debbie's mother and I would like to welcome you," he told the room. "We're grateful you're here to celebrate with us, and especially grateful to the Baileys for supplying the venue." (I was glad he'd thought to mention that.) "Most important, though: I hope you'll all join us in wishing Kenneth and Debbie the very happiest of marriages."

Every one of us murmured agreement to that one.

Here the toasts were supposed to end, according to Sophie's index card, but a lot of people didn't know that and so several of them stood up to make spontaneous toasts of their own, sometimes unintentionally preempting other people who'd taken it into their heads to stand up at the very same moment. Bitsy Taylor announced that she'd been the first to realize, on the very evening when Kenneth and Debbie were introduced, that they were meant for each other. Dave the usher told us that "Change the name and not the letter, change for worse and not for better" was completely not the case with Deborah Baines Bailey. (Since Debbie would be keeping her maiden name, this didn't seem all that relevant.) Even Spofford Talbot had something to say. He spoke up from a far corner of the room where he had retreated, hugging his camera, to call out, "Thanks for posing, all," in a surprisingly deep voice. ("Who was *that*?" several people asked each other.)

Then Sophie consulted her index card one last time and said, "Tossing of the bouquet!" At which point Cyndi Lauper burst out with "Girls Just Want to Have Fun" while various young women—not only the bridal attendants but also young women from other tables—rose to gather around Debbie in the center of the room. I hadn't realized that mere guests could be involved. The one who caught the bouquet was a little sprite of a redhead who merely reached out and snagged it nonchalantly. In fact, the whole production lacked any sense of urgency. "In *my* day," my mother said, "girls would scramble all over themselves trying to catch the bouquet."

"Yes, well, that was then," Sophie said with a sigh.

I could tell that this whole event had fallen far short of what she thought a wedding should be.

She and Rupert had done way more than their part, though. I did realize that. Max and I were hardly more than bystanders. So later, as we began heading toward the exit, I went up to her and said, "Thank you, Sophie. I wouldn't have known the first thing about how to arrange all this."

"Why, you're welcome, my dear!" Sophie said. I got the feeling that she was surprised I'd had the good manners to say anything. "It did go well, I thought," she said. "And upon reflection, I can understand why they had plain old roses on their cake instead of a bride and groom. A bride doll in white satin would not have gone with Debbie's outfit in the *least*!"

Sometimes when I find out what's on other people's minds I honestly wonder if we all live on totally separate planets.

Like Jared, for instance. While the first group of leavetakers was waiting for the elevator—Max and Mom and I among them—Jared came up to me and said, "So. Gail. May I call you?"

"Call about what?" I asked.

"I had thought we might go out sometime. Go out to dinner, say."

"Oh. I don't know," I told him. "I'm not really all that social."

"I see."

"Sorry," I said.

"That's okay!" He turned abruptly toward an older woman standing nearby. "Millie Decker! How've you *been*?" he asked in a loud voice, and then the elevator doors slid open and I boarded, followed by Max and my mother. Jared, however, held back, even though there was plenty of room. "Told you so," Mom said to me under her breath.

I pretended not to hear her. And I was careful not to look at Max. I said, "You-all don't think this is the last we'll see of Debbie, do you?"

"The last we'll see of her forever?" Mom asked.

"No, Mom. The last time tonight. Are we going to see her again downstairs?"

"I kind of doubt it," Max said. "It looked to me like she was still caught up with some of those gals from the bouquet tossing."

"Darn," I said. "I wanted to tell her good-bye."

"So give her a call tomorrow. They're not leaving till afternoon, remember."

"I can't phone the day after their wedding!"

"Why not?"

"It would be intrusive!"

The elevator landed so smoothly that I had to look up at the panel of numbers to make sure we had arrived. "Where will they be going?" Mom asked as we stepped out.

"Bermuda. Their plane leaves at two or so."

"Well, she's right," Mom told Max. "Even if they're in town still, you wouldn't want to disturb their privacy."

"Suit yourself," Max said with a shrug.

Our crowd fanned out across the dim parking garage. I had no idea where the car was; it seemed to me we'd parked days ago. But Max headed toward it unerringly, and Mom and I followed.

Once we had settled in our seats, I told Max, "I was thinking we'd all be leaving the club in a bunch, and that's when we'd tell her good-bye."

"I guess I was thinking the same," he said. He plucked the parking receipt from above his sun visor, meanwhile inching behind a stream of taillights toward the exit. "And also, of course, Kenneth," he said.

"Kenneth?"

"Telling Kenneth . . ." He rolled down his window to feed the ticket into a slot. "Telling him, I don't know, just to take good care of our daughter, I guess." He was quiet a moment. Then he said, "Remember after *our* wedding?"

"We didn't have a—"

"Remember how we went to your folkses' house afterward to let them know? *You* remember, Joyce. And your dad took me aside and told me that any time you did something that just completely baffled me, I should come to him and he would explain it."

In the backseat, my mother snorted. "I'd like to hear what he would have said," she told Max.

But I didn't even need to consider. "He'd say, 'Well, she's always been difficult.'"

Max laughed. My mother, though, was quiet. "Oh, my," she sighed after a moment. "Wouldn't he have loved to watch his granddaughter get married!"

After that, all three of us were quiet.

We exited the parking garage into semi-twilight, onto streets giving off a gray sheen although it wasn't actively raining. Other cars passed with a faint hissing sound, including one long, sleek, silver sedan that I thought might hold Reverend Gregory and his wife, although I couldn't be certain.

When we drew up in front of Mom's apartment building, she said, "Thank you for the ride, Max."

"You're welcome," he told her.

Then she turned to me and said, "Now, don't you go feeling sad, you hear?"

"No, I'm okay," I said.

"It was a lovely, lovely wedding," she said, "and you should be very proud of her."

"I *am* proud."

What I mainly felt, though, was flatness. As soon as we were on our own I slumped down in my seat, and Max may have felt the same way. In any case, neither of us said a word for the rest of the drive home.

⁓⁓

Just inside my front door, the cat stood waiting for us like a parent enforcing a curfew. She meowed crossly as soon as we entered and then she turned away and stalked off toward the kitchen. The implication was that she was merely concerned about her food supply, but I knew better. "You can't fool *me*," I told her. "You missed us, didn't you."

Even so, I followed her. There was still kibble in her bowl, as I'd expected, but since I was in the kitchen anyhow I called, "Max? You want a beer?"

"That'd be good," he said.

I brought him one, along with a glass of wine for myself. It was true that I had grumbled when I learned he'd be staying at my house, but I did feel kind of relieved now to have someone to rehash the wedding with. I sat down on the couch and kicked my shoes off. Max had already shed his suit coat, and he was settled in the recliner, tipped as far back as he could go. He took a long swallow of beer and said, "Ah, me."

"Well, we survived," I said.

"We did, it seems."

We listened to the crunching sound of kibble in the kitchen.

"I wonder how much I'll have to see of Sophie in the coming years," I said.

"Now, now, she's not so bad."

"Easy for *you* to say. You're off on the Eastern Shore."

"You have the matrilineal advantage, though," he told me.

"The what?"

"It's a term I heard on the radio this morning. The mother of the wife gets dibs on the family holidays, most often, and she tends to see more of her grandchildren than the mother of the husband does."

"But you told me Kenneth was going to expect Debbie to spend the holidays with *his* family."

"That was before I listened to WYPR," Max said.

"Ah," I said. I took a sip of my wine. "And were you as surprised as I was," I asked, "that Sophie didn't bat an eye at the word 'ass' in Elizabeth's toast?"

"Well, she does live in the modern world," Max said. "I doubt it was the first time she'd heard it." Then he grinned. "And your mother handled it fine, I noticed."

"Yes, Mom lives in the modern world too," I said. "Even though she doesn't always seem to."

I tilted my head back against the back of the couch. "In fact, it was kind of a shock that that toast even happened," I said. "That Elizabeth decided to do it, I mean."

"Oh, well," Max said. "They're a family. Families get over these things."

"Not always."

The cat came ambling out of the kitchen. I heard her footsteps even before she sprang onto the couch to settle beside me.

"For a while there," I told the ceiling, "I had thought we'd get through the whole wedding with the groom and the maid of honor not speaking."

"I don't imagine it would have been the first time," Max said.

"And did it seem to you that Kenneth got a little teary, there at the end?" I asked.

"Yep. I thought so too."

"Which doesn't for one minute mean he's not guilty, of course."

I heard a slamming sound, and I lifted my head. Max had just returned his recliner to its fully upright position. "Give it a rest, Gail," he told me.

"What?"

"Of course he's guilty."

I stared at him.

"Read between the lines," he said. "He's guilty but Debbie forgave him, and now it's over and done with."

"So you agree that his food-poisoning story—"

"He made that story up, and Debbie chose to believe it. Or she *didn't* believe it, so he broke down and confessed and she forgave him. Or—and here's the one I'm hoping for—he confessed right off and she forgave him right off, and then the two of them hatched that story together to put a good face on things. Whichever. It's none of our business."

"You make it sound so simple," I said.

"It *is* simple. And one thing I know for certain is, she's sorry as hell now she told us about it and she's hoping we will never bring it up again."

I thought this over.

"So," I said finally, "it seems I'm the only one who still holds Kenneth accountable."

"Right," he said. "Ironic, isn't it."

"Ironic?" I said. "What?"

But all at once, he got very busy. He stood up and took a quick slug of his beer and said, "Well, I guess I'll turn in now," and went to the kitchen with his can. When he came out he said, "Good night," and headed straight up the stairs.

"Good night," I said.

Ironic?

Because I hadn't forgiven Kenneth even though Debbie had,

I guessed. But more than that: because I *of all people* hadn't forgiven him.

I wasn't the least bit sleepy, but eventually I stood up too and went to pour the last of my wine down the kitchen sink. Then I turned off all the downstairs lights and went to bed.

three

THE DAY AFTER

Very early on Sunday morning, so early it was barely light out, I woke not by degrees but all at once. I just *found* myself awake—wham!—with the cool damp nose of a cat daintily probing my left ear.

Oh.

The cat.

I turned onto my back, and the cat started purring and settled herself in her favorite spot next to my ribcage.

It's over, I thought. Debbie's wedding day is over, thank God. And really it all went fine.

She was probably still asleep now, on this very first day of her marriage. I didn't feel any sense of envy. What person in her right mind would want to go back to being a newlywed? There was so much she had yet to adjust to, she and Kenneth both; I was just glad to be past all that.

Once upon a time, Debbie had sworn she would never get married. Back in fifth grade, this was. Never, ever, she had said. She'd have to be crazy to get married. That was my fault entirely; I knew it even then. I'd fallen in love with another man that year and torn our family apart forever.

His name was Andrew Mason. He was the college admissions counselor at Millwood High, where I taught algebra and remedial math. A medium-height, medium-weight man in his late forties. Short brown hair, pale gray eyes, and a complicated mouth that made his smiles seem slightly held back, slightly reluctant, in an appealing sort of way. He always wore a suit to work, but he wore it casually, as if merely to satisfy some requirement, and his shirt was open collared, without a tie.

I met him on his first day at Millwood, at the start of the 2000–2001 school year. He'd been hired to replace June Cannon, who'd retired the previous spring at the age of (I'm guessing here) a hundred and five. As I was walking back from Bert's Beans, where I'd just bought the takeout coffee that I liked to begin my day with, he pulled up next to me in a little beige Volkswagen Beetle. "Excuse me," he called out his window. "Are you familiar with this area?"

"Yes," I said.

"Would you happen to know if there's a grownups' lot around here for Millwood High?"

"A grownups' lot."

"The parking lot behind the school seems to be just for students, and I can't find any grownup parking."

"Oh," I said, "the kids must've been tinkering with the sign again. It's supposed to say '*No* Student Parking,' but they keep painting over the 'No.' You'll be fine there."

"Thanks," he said.

And both of us went on our way.

I guessed even then that he might be the new college admissions counselor. So I wasn't surprised to see him in the front hall that afternoon, tacking a notice up on the bulletin board. "Hi there!" he said, and I said, "Hi," and gave him a wave.

The notice—as I saw when I passed by again later—announced the specific hours when students could come talk to him without a prior appointment. I thought that showed good sense. June Cannon's office had been sheer chaos, from the looks of it.

I didn't see him again until a couple of days after that. I'd stopped by the school library to check the Recent Acquisitions shelf, and I found him doing the same. He turned and raised his eyebrows and smiled. "It appears you're following me," he said.

"I can understand why you'd think so," I told him, "but that must have been my twin sister."

I have no idea what led me to say that. Well, I do have *some* idea: it was the first time I'd seen that smile of his, that smile-in-spite-of-itself, and I wanted to make it grow wider. Which it did, in fact. It turned into an actual grin. "My mistake," he said.

And then we kind of tilted our chins at each other, acknowledging the joke, and I went back to my classroom.

At the end of school hours that Friday, he happened to walk past my office. I had a tiny office of my own that was separate from my classroom—no more than a cubbyhole, really—where I could meet with my remedial students one-on-one, and I was just collecting some papers for the weekend when he paused outside the door. "I should have introduced myself before," he told me. "I'm Andrew Mason."

"Hi, Andrew. I'm Gail Baines."

"Yes, I know you are," he said, and he took a step in to survey the room, such as it was. Behind my desk was a low bookshelf holding files and half a dozen framed photos—Debbie in a kiddie pool, Debbie and I at a playground, Debbie and Max and I at my parents' anniversary party. Andrew circled the desk to look at these. Then he said, "I don't see your twin sister."

"Oh, she's here," I said, and I pointed to the playground picture. "This one's her."

"No, it's not," he said. "It's you. I can tell by that little white scar on your chin."

He was talking about the half-inch line, no wider than a thread, that ran vertically from just above my jawbone to just below it. (A roller-skating injury from childhood.) I was surprised he'd even spotted it. I said, "Actually, we both have that. I got mine first, and then she cut one on her own chin so we could still match."

"Tisk, tisk," he said, giving the word an ironic pronunciation. "A *copycat* twin." He picked up the playground photo and examined it more closely. "Very unoriginal of her."

"I won't tell you which is which in the others," I said. And the odd thing was that as I stood gazing at the photos myself, I really did feel all at once that they showed two different women.

Which was the case throughout the time I knew him, it strikes me now. Two completely different women: one who loved her husband the same as always, and another who wanted to reach out a finger and very, very gently nudge this man's smile a smidgen higher at the corners.

It could have gone either way from there. He could have become a good friend who went to the symphony sometimes with Max and me, just like Morrie Gray from the science department. But somehow, I don't know . . . For one thing, our encounters happened to take place in private, for the most part. Andrew never ate in the cafeteria, where the teachers gathered in a chatty bunch at a single long table, because noon was one of the times he kept open for drop-in students. Nor did he attend the Friday-morning assemblies; it wasn't part of his job description. Generally, we'd just fall into step with each other in the parking lot or the front hall corridor. We would both slow down and I might ask how he was settling in (very well, he always said), or he might add some new embellishment to our twin myth. Then gradually he developed the habit of stopping by my office to ask for my advice on how to deal with our difficult principal, or where to take his sister to dinner when she came for a visit. He might even settle on the chair opposite my desk for a moment, if our discussion grew more involved.

He was divorced, and he had no children. The divorce had happened some years ago; the marriage had been brief and—I sensed—lacking in impact. His ex-wife lived in Virginia now with her current husband and their three daughters. He had never wanted children himself, he said; just hadn't developed the urge, somehow. He lived in a small house in Pimlico, and he referred often to his yard—what fall colors his bushes were changing to and what he thought he might plant next spring—so I gathered he was the gardening type. Which I was not, most emphatically, and neither was Max.

I did mention him to Max, but not in any detail. I might quote something Andrew had said that had amused me, but then I'd move on to discuss the new basketball coach or the latest feud among the English teachers.

Max was dealing with his own issues at the time. He was threatening to quit his job at St. Theresa because they focused too much on religion. "It's a religious *school*, for gosh sake," I said, but he said, "They still shouldn't be meddling with my reading list." And so on and so forth. The point is, Max was not fully present right then.

But I realize that's no excuse.

I confided to Andrew that the trouble with Max was, he didn't take things seriously. He didn't take *himself* seriously. He had a tendency to wander off course halfway through a project, as if his life were just a casual experiment.

"I think most of the world works that way," Andrew told me. "People look at where they've arrived and say, 'Huh! So *that's* how it is!' as if they themselves had nothing to do with it."

"Right," I said. "They're so . . . accepting."

Andrew smiled. He said, "You say that as if it's a shortcoming."

"Well, sometimes it is," I said.

Andrew's office was on the first floor. So was mine, but my classroom was on the second floor. Anytime I came downstairs to confer with a student in my office I would feel this acute consciousness, this prickly awareness in the back of my neck as I walked past Andrew's closed door.

When I imagined becoming involved with him—not that I really would! I told myself. Not that I'd actually do such a thing!—I pictured its happening in my cubbyhole. He would stop by and we'd get to talking and then gradually we would fall silent; we would look at each other across my desk; we would know what the other was thinking. Or he would catch up with me in the parking lot and, "Gail," he would say, "we have to talk," and then he'd take hold of my arm and lead me to my car. Or I would just be turning my key in the ignition when I heard his tap on my driver's-side window.

But in fact it happened in my classroom, in my big sunny open classroom with its bank of giant picture windows and its seating for thirty-two students. I was eating lunch at my desk one day because I had a stack of exams to grade before the next period began. I was feeding myself a spoonful of yogurt when I chanced to look up and notice him in my doorway. Just standing in my doorway, watching me. He might have been there for some time. He said, "How long can we keep this up, Gail?"

I had to finish dragging my plastic spoon upside-down along the length of my tongue before I could answer him. I had to swallow. It was awkward. Then I said, "I don't know how long."

What I *should* have said was, "We can keep this up forever. We can go on leaving things unspoken, letting them teeter in the balance, because isn't everything perfect just the way it is?"

But I didn't.

※

In my earlier life, my pre-marriage life, my few scant romances had proceeded as if by mere chance. A guy and I would get close and then closer, and then on the spur of the moment off to bed we'd go. But not anymore, of course. Now we had to make an appointment ahead of time.

Or *I* had to make an appointment. Not so much Andrew. Andrew's life was spare and orderly. Mine was cluttered. Andrew worked from eight thirty to three, five days a week. I also worked from eight thirty to three, but in addition I had a husband and a daughter to see to. Carpools, playdates, pediatrician appointments . . . It didn't leave a lot of room for romantic assignations. In fact, we had to wait three days that first time before we could finally be together. Wednesday, Thursday, Friday. On Friday, Debbie would be spending the night with a friend from her school. It was her very first overnight, and she kept checking with me on Friday morning to make certain I would rescue her if she got homesick. "I can call you if I need to, right?" she asked. "I mean, like even if it's the middle of the night I can call and you will come for me."

"Yes, of course," I said, because by then I would have been home for hours. I had to fix supper for Max, after all. "I'll come in my pajamas, if I have to."

"Or, but, if I'm just getting into Pam's mom's car after school and I change my mind then, I can call too, right?"

"Right," I said, but more faintly. "Although it might be harder to reach me then. You might have to go on home with Pam and I would pick you up a bit later."

It was Max who drove Debbie to school every morning, because their schools started later than mine did. But even as I was walking out of the house she was hanging on to my wrist and saying, "You promise? You won't tell me I should try to stay there when I don't want to, will you?"

"I would never do that," I said. And I meant it.

But she managed the whole thing just fine, it turned out. She and I had both worried for no reason.

The plan was that at the end of my school day, I would follow Andrew home in my car. I followed him past the Pimlico racetrack and then northward on a series of little neighborhood streets until we reached a small white cottage with yellowish stains descending from the eaves and all the windowsills. The yard, though, was meticulously cared for. Grass like a flawless green velvet carpet, a row of flowerpots in graduated sizes marching down the steps from the stoop, and a dwarf Japanese maple out front with leaves that glowed magenta. When I stepped out of my car my first words were "Is all this *your* doing?" So of course Andrew had to give me the garden tour, leading me around back so he could show me his little vegetable plot with its abundance of acorn squash and zucchini even this late in the fall. "Mm-hmm, I see," I kept saying, and, "Goodness! Look at the *size* of those!" but inwardly, I was worrying I'd worn the wrong underwear. It was black, and very lacy—too obvious, I realized. I should have worn plain white, as if I'd given the subject no thought. ("And are those bushes lilacs?" I asked.) Actually, I told myself, it wasn't mandatory that we should have sex on this very first occasion. In fact, I'd prefer not to. I would put him off; I would say I wasn't ready. I would suggest we meet again next Tuesday, when Debbie had gymnastics practice. We wouldn't have as much time then—I had to pick her up at five—but it was manageable. And I would wear white underwear, except that my bra would be the extra-nice one with the seashell-shaped cups.

We went inside. (Neat as a pin, but a bit too sparsely furnished. His ex-wife had taken all the best pieces, he said.) In the kitchen I stalled a bit by pausing to run an index finger across the spines of his cookbooks, but that proved unnecessary because next he offered to make coffee. "I'd *love* some coffee!" I said.

"Is decaf okay?" he asked.

"Decaf is perfect."

"I can't sleep a wink if I drink real coffee after ten a.m.," he said, and I said, "Ten! Well, that *is* early. I have real coffee with my lunch, lots of times, but I wouldn't want to risk it any later in the day."

I don't know why I was speaking so loudly.

He filled his coffeemaker with water and ladled the decaf in with a measuring spoon. Meanwhile I found the sugar bowl in a cabinet and set it at the center of the table. My scheme was that we should have our coffee in the kitchen. Kitchens were more... vertical than living rooms.

I looked in the fridge for cream (a nicely stocked fridge; he must actually cook), but when I didn't find any I took out the milk instead. He was probably one of those people who think cream is unhealthy. I poured the milk into a cream pitcher and placed it on the table next to the sugar bowl. Andrew, meanwhile, was watching the coffeemaker burbling away, his focus so intent you'd think it couldn't have functioned without his gaze.

"Silverware?" I asked, and he turned toward the table then and said, "Oh!" I thought at first he was surprised I hadn't set things up in the living room, but what he said next was, "I'm sorry you went to all that trouble. I happen to take my coffee black."

I said, "*I* don't, though."

"Oh, right."

"Where will I find the spoons?" I asked him.

He gestured toward a drawer.

"And napkins?" I said.

"There beside the toaster."

The napkins were white linen, stacked in a wickerwork box. Aha, a conversational topic. "I'm impressed," I told him. "Max and I just use paper, I'm ashamed to say."

Clumsy of me to mention Max. It was habit; that was all.

"The fact is, I like to iron," Andrew told me.

"I know what you mean!" I said. "I love to iron."

"You do?"

"It's like you get an instant *effect* when you iron."

"Exactly. Things start out all screwed-up and crinkled—"

"But then sudden, perfect smoothness."

"And I don't believe in steam irons," Andrew said.

"No, you want to really soak things," I said. "Do you own an actual sprinkler bottle?"

"I *do* own a sprinkler bottle!" Andrew said.

We smiled at each other. The coffeemaker stopped burbling, but he just stood there smiling at me. So it was up to me to step forward, finally, and wrap my arms around him and press the length of my body against him and lift my face to his.

After that, he was the one in charge. He drew away from me and took my hand and led me out of the kitchen, and through the foyer, and up the stairs.

※

It was hard to find places to meet during the run of a normal day. We had my little office, of course, and Andrew's larger one; but both of those felt so public, even with the doors closed. We couldn't really *do* anything. Better to drive separately during lunch hour to this little dog park nearby that nobody else seemed to know about, and grab a hurried twenty minutes together. Better yet, of course, to wait for one of Debbie's gymnastics days or her after-school playdates when I could go to his house again. But I never took him to my own house, because that would have felt disloyal.

Yes, I know: it was disloyal of me anyplace. But it seemed more so in the house I shared with Max.

Once Andrew said, "Gail? Do you ever think about . . . making this more permanent? Splitting up with Max, someday?"

"Splitting," I said.

"I don't mean this very minute. I know we'd have to wait for the right time, what with your daughter and all."

As if there could ever be a right time to do such a thing to a child! We'd have to wait till Debbie was forty.

But the answer to his question (an answer I never actually voiced) was yes, I thought about it a lot. I thought about waking up with him every morning, going to sleep with him every night, weaving my life into that measured, considered routine of his where the potted plants descended the steps in the proper order and everything happened according to a plan. I ached for it.

He and I were a couple for exactly ninety-six days. Mid-September till shortly before Christmas. Not quite fourteen weeks.

On Tuesday, December 19, Debbie had gymnastics practice. And I was at Andrew's, with my internal alarm clock set for 4:45 p.m. so I could get to Debbie's school in time to pick her up at five.

Somewhere around four o'clock, Debbie dislocated her shoulder doing a dismount from the uneven bars. Her school called me at home and got no answer, so they called Max at St. Theresa. (Neither one of us owned a cell phone, back then.) And Max got someone to cover the after-school study hall he monitored so he could collect Debbie and take her to the ER, which was where I found them both when I drove there directly from her school. They were still in the waiting room, because this was Sinai Hospital, where things always took forever. Debbie seemed more concerned about her future gymnastics career than about any pain she was feeling, and Max had been through a couple of dislocations himself so he took it all pretty calmly. I was by far the most upset. "I'm sorry!" I told them both as I rushed up to them. "I'm so sorry! I was just—I took a drive in the country, and I had no *idea* this had happened!"

Stupid, stupid. When had I ever in my life taken a drive alone in the country for no good reason? I should have said I'd been running errands; that would have been more believable. But Max was so unsuspecting; all he said was, "No harm done. They've already had a peek at her and they say the doctor can fix her up as good as new."

I sank down on the chair next to Debbie and gave her a hug, avoiding her shoulder. I was out of breath and shaky. "Are you okay?" I asked her.

"I'm *fine*, Mom."

"I feel awful," I told Max.

"Why?" he asked me. "Sweetheart. This is nothing; believe me."

"I know, I know..."

Then they called Debbie's name, and the three of us stood up and followed a nurse into an examining room.

Once we were home again, finally—at almost eight p.m., all three of us starving to death—Debbie had to telephone every friend she could think of and give them the gory details. Meanwhile I heated up some frozen tacos and Max tossed a salad. He had put the whole incident behind him by that time. He was telling me about a protest meeting he was planning with a few other teachers at St. Theresa. And I was saying, "Mm-hmm, yes; well, of course you do . . ." But inwardly I was sick at heart. I couldn't believe I had been cavorting in bed with some near stranger while my husband and my daughter went to the emergency room without me.

Immediately after supper, while Max was loading the dishwasher, I ducked into the den where we kept the computer and sent Andrew an email. *I can't see you anymore*, I wrote. *I'm sorry.* I didn't even bother explaining; that's how eager I was to get the whole thing over with. Then I shut down the computer quick-quick and was back in the kitchen in time to wipe the table and turn off the lights.

I lay awake for hours that night. We were living in Roland Park at the time, but not in the fancy part, and I could hear the traffic from Cold Spring Lane and the occasional hoots of Loyola students heading home from the bars. Max, beside me, slept almost without moving. Maybe he'd found Debbie's accident more draining than he had let on. And I didn't hear a peep from Debbie's room.

I wondered if Andrew had answered my email yet, or if instead he planned to wait till we could talk about it face-to-face. Or maybe we'd *never* talk about it. Maybe he would accept my decision in silence and back off gracefully. That was what I hoped for.

I could have gotten up and gone downstairs to check the computer, but I couldn't bear to deal with one more issue just now.

I did fall asleep, finally, and woke much later than I should have. Max was already up; I could hear Debbie chattering away to him down in the kitchen. So I washed and dressed in a hurry, and I ducked into the kitchen just long enough to ask her how her shoulder felt (sore, she said) and to give her and Max a peck on the cheek before I rushed off, grabbing my jacket from the coat closet on my way.

"Don't forget I have a meeting this afternoon," Max called after me.

"I remember," I called back, even though I hadn't.

For the past few weeks I had chosen my clothes so carefully, always with an eye to how Andrew might judge them, but on that particular morning I wore the outfit I'd worn the day before, knit slacks and a gray sweater, although the sweater was the kind where the neck gets stretchy after one wearing and it really should have gone in the wash.

Andrew's VW was already parked in the lot, and when I walked past his office door I could hear the rumbling of his voice, either talking on the phone or in conference with somebody's parents. It was still homeroom period, the principal's announcements still crackling over the PA system, but first bell rang even before I reached my classroom. A few of my students—the loners and the misfits, the ones without a gang of friends to horse around with in the hall—were already at their desks, and more started trickling in by twos and threes, nodding at me as they entered but seldom answering my "Good morning." I made a business of draping my jacket over the back of my chair and stowing my purse in a bottom drawer, and by that time second bell had rung and I went out to the hall to round up the last stragglers.

Except that Max was in the hall.

Max stood in front of me, not even wearing his jacket, his face grayish white and stony.

"*What*," I said. I grabbed hold of him with both hands. "What's happened? Is it Debbie? Where's Debbie?"

"Debbie's still home," he said. He seemed to speak without moving his lips.

"Is she all right?"

"She's fine."

"Then what—?"

"See him how?" he asked me.

I stared at him.

"See Andrew how? How did you mean that, 'can't see you'?"

I dropped my hands.

"What's going on, Gail?" he asked me.

I couldn't find words.

"Are you having a . . . ? Is this some kind of . . . *affair*? Is that what you meant?"

"No, I—"

"Just tell me it's nothing," he said.

"It's nothing!"

"Then why did you write that?"

"I just meant—"

"Is this why we don't have sex anymore?"

That was the question that made me aware, finally, of the roomful of students behind me. To this day I'm not sure if they heard him. All I remember is rushing back into the room for my belongings and rushing out again, not even looking in their direction; but I suspect (I hope) they were oblivious, too busy with their own all-absorbing lives to pay any attention to mine. I don't think I even closed the door behind me. I snatched a handful of Max's sleeve and pulled him along. It felt like dragging a reluctant dog. I pulled him toward the stairs, I pulled him down to the first floor. "This is not what it looks like," I told him. "You have it all wrong."

He halted outside on the front stoop and wrested his arm away. "What is it, then, Gail?" he asked.

"He's just a friend," I told him. "You've misunderstood."

"'I can't see you anymore,' you said. What else could that mean?"

"You had no business whatsoever reading my private mail," I told him.

"It was sitting right there on the screen, already open!"

"This is what happens to people who—what?"

"I was going to send out a reminder about this afternoon's protest meeting and there it was, just sitting on the screen waiting to be sent."

"It hadn't been sent?"

"I need you to explain," he said.

But instead of waiting for my explanation, he turned and walked on down the front steps, out toward the parking lot. I had to run to keep up with him. When he reached his car he got in and immediately started the engine, but he neglected to unlock the passenger door, either accidentally or on purpose. I had to rap on the side window frantically till he leaned over and raised the button. And I wasn't even properly settled in my seat before he pulled out of his parking space.

"*You* know how it is," I told him. "You have a friend who talks on and on about his troubles and whatnot; sometimes you just think, *Enough!* And so you tell him—"

Max drove silently, looking straight ahead of him. It wasn't any use.

"I'm sorry," I said. "I am so, so sorry."

He said, "Are you going to leave me?"

"No!" I said. And then, when he didn't react: "I told him! You saw what I told him; I said I couldn't see him anymore."

"But you didn't say, 'I don't *want* to see you.'"

"Well, I don't," I said.

We turned onto Cold Spring Lane. There was some kind of roadwork happening, men in bulky jackets conferring around an excavation in the middle of the pavement. We had to come to a stop for a while. The silence in the car was something I could almost touch, like a curtain.

"Debbie's not in school?" I asked belatedly.

"I left her at home," he said.

One of the workers gestured us forward, and Max maneuvered around him and drove on.

I said, "She's not going in today?"

"I'll take her later."

So we were missing in action, all three of us. Debbie late for school, Max and I ditching our classes. My car was abandoned in the Millwood parking lot. My students were unattended, and probably raising a ruckus. But none of that seemed important.

I wanted to say something. There was so much I wanted to say. But I made myself wait till we could have a solid block of time.

When we got home, Debbie was watching TV in the den. "Where *were* you?" she asked Max, and then to me, "Why aren't you at work?"

"Sorry, hon," was all Max said. "Grab your backpack and let's hit the road."

Her backpack was already waiting beside the front door. Max had to help with her jacket, though, because of her shoulder. He slid her good arm into one sleeve and then zipped the jacket shut around her other arm in its sling. "Have a nice day!" I said, giving her a hug.

"Bye, Mom."

The instant they were gone, I walked into the den and turned on the computer. *i cant see you anymore im sorry*, the screen told me. I sent it off without a thought and shut down the computer. Then I reached for the phone and called Millwood. Told the secretary I'd been struck by a violent stomach bug and apologized for not giving more notice.

I think I half assumed that Max would come back to the house once he'd delivered Debbie, and that was when we'd have our talk. Hash it all out. Clear the air. But he didn't come back. He went on with his normal day, evidently, while I sat miserably at home. When he failed to show up even during his lunch hour, I risked leaving the house just long enough to take a cab to Millwood so I could collect my car. Needless to say, I was careful not to be seen. I ducked behind the wheel like a thief; I drove home at record speed. There was no sign that Max had been there during my absence, thank God. In fact he stayed away even for his after-school study hall and his after-after-school protest meeting. Debbie and I had to wait supper. Debbie was begging to start without him, but I said, "Just a teeny bit longer, okay?" Privately, I was frantic. When he finally arrived, though, all he said was, "Well, *that* was a waste of time. Nobody wants to rock the boat, as it turns out."

"Oh, what a pity," I said.

"A bunch of scaredy-cats."

I've never been gladder in my life to chitchat about a protest meeting.

But after supper, after Debbie had gone upstairs to do her homework, I went into the den where Max was watching the news. I sat quietly beside him until a commercial came on, and then I said, "Max."

"Hmm?"

"Can we talk?"

"Not right now, hon. I'm bushed," he said.

Should I have insisted? I still don't know the answer.

Because from that time on, Max behaved as if nothing whatsoever had happened. For the following days and weeks and months it was *Everything's fine!* and *What could possibly be wrong?* He was his usual good-natured self. He was blithely, blandly cheerful.

Except...

Except he didn't think I hung the moon anymore.

Yes, I know this was what I deserved. But still, I felt crushed, and all the more so because everything was unspoken. Max simply did not speak of it. Our lives proceeded as pleasantly and uneventfully as always.

Andrew, on the other hand...

On Thursday morning, when I returned to work, Andrew knocked at my cubbyhole just before second period. "Gail," he said, the instant I opened the door, "what is it? Did Max find out about us?"

I *despised* that question! So gossipy, so intrusive. And what right did he have to call Max by his first name? They hadn't even met! It was all I could do to say, "Yes, Andrew, he did. Sorry; I meant what I said in my email." Then I shut the door in his face.

After that, we were two strangers. We said, "Good morning," in the hallway. And in the spring, when he began to be seen around and about with Mamie Fox from the Spanish department, I felt nothing but relief. It was as if he had been burned out of me. Seared out. There was nothing left of him.

It did occur to me that it might be fear that made me feel this way—fear of losing everything I valued most—and I wondered if maybe much later I would allow myself to mourn him. But in fact, that never happened. I forgot about him, basically, and in the rare moments when he came to mind I wondered what had ever drawn me to him. Why had I, who truly loved my husband—at least in the on-again-off-again, maybe/maybe-not, semi-happy way of just about any married woman—broken apart my whole world for a man I never really knew? But maybe that was just it: I hadn't known him. There are times when that can be the strongest draw of all.

~~~

I hadn't expected to get back to sleep, but suddenly my eyes were blinking open again and the cat was long gone and the sun was casting bright yellow squares across my bedspread. Why couldn't we have had this weather for the wedding? I got up and went to raise the window. It was cooler outside than in but still humid, so I lowered the window again.

By the time I was dressed, I could hear Max moving around downstairs. I found him emptying the litter box into the garbage container under the sink while the cat wove in and out around his ankles. "Morning!" he said, straightening. He gestured toward the garbage container. "Don't worry; I'll carry this out right after breakfast."

"How long have you been up?" I asked him.

"Not that long."

"Are you about to take off?"

"Take off?"

"For the Eastern Shore?"

"No, no, it's Sunday. Not much need for an early start on a Sunday."

Sunday was *exactly* when you'd want an early start. Traffic would get heavier hour by hour until evening. But I didn't point that out. I said, "So, what would you like for breakfast?"

"Why don't I fix us something. How'd you sleep?"

"Like a rock," I said, "At least, till the crack of dawn. How about you?"

He said, "I dreamed about Debbie."

"Good or bad?" I asked.

"I dreamed she came and told us she wanted to go back to college and would we be willing to pay for it. And we said, 'What're you planning to study?' and she said, 'Well, I've always secretly wished that I were a beautician.' So we said—"

And there he went, ambling down the rabbit hole of his dream as he carried the litter box back to the powder room. I could hear him pouring in fresh litter, and it struck me that doing this so shortly before he left was suspicious timing. Surely he didn't imagine I might decide to keep the cat after all? But that was Max for you. Sixty-five years old, and yet he still believed that human beings were capable of change.

Once again, though, I held my tongue. I started a pot of coffee brewing, and when he came back to the kitchen he took the egg carton from the fridge.

"I was thinking I might go over to the school and collect my things," I told him.

"What things?"

"The stuff in my desk and all."

He turned from the stove. He said, "So you were serious? You really are planning to quit?"

"I might as well," I said with a shrug.

"But you don't have anything else lined up yet."

"Ha! How many times have *you* quit a job with nothing else lined up?"

"That's different," he said. "I'm not the worrying type." He dropped a pat of butter into the frying pan. "Besides, you can't just waltz into school on a Sunday and abscond with all your belongings and never be heard from again."

"Why not? What can they do, fire me?"

He gave a grudging little hiss of a laugh.

I filled two glasses with orange juice and set them on the table. Then I got out the bread and put two slices in the toaster.

"You know what?" Max said. "Later today, I'm going to phone Levy."

"Who's Levy?"

"The head of my school. I'm going to ask if he has a job for you."

"Max."

"You'd love it there! It's got these really nice students, needy students; they've just had a bad break, is all. Enough of those rich-kid types you've been dealing with."

"It's not *their* fault they're rich," I said mildly. "Besides: I bet there's a rule of some kind against hiring relatives."

"You and I are not relatives, though," Max pointed out.

"Oh," I said. "Right."

"And once you show Levy your references, he'll be dying to hire you."

"Not if Marilee mentions the people-skills thing."

"People skills, schmeeple skills," Max said, and he rapped his spatula sharply against the rim of the frying pan.

I was a little bit disappointed. You would think he could have come up with a better rebuttal than that.

He turned off the burner and brought the frying pan to the table. His eggs looked like a puff of pale yellow clouds. I said, "Is it okay that we're eating all these scrambled eggs and omelets and such?"

"Why wouldn't it be?" he asked.

"Aren't they bad for our cholesterol or something?"

"That was last week," he told me. "Everything's changed." He dished out a serving for me and then put the other half on his own plate. Meanwhile, I got up to retrieve the toast from the toaster. "Face it, though," he said. "You'll have a better chance of being hired if you don't have a break-and-enter on your record."

"It wouldn't *literally* be breaking and entering," I said. "I do own a key, you realize."

"Even so," he said.

"Maybe I should just give up on teaching and sell asparagus instead."

"You jest," he told me, "but it's true the pay might be better." He started spreading butter on his toast, about a quarter-inch thick. (Talk about cholesterol!) "However, I'd hate to deprive our students of such a talented teacher," he said.

"Why, thank you," I said.

The phone rang.

"Who is it?" Max asked me.

I rose to check the caller ID. I said, "Oh!" and snatched up the receiver. "Debbie?" I said.

"Hi, Mom."

Max set his toast down.

"Is—?" I said. I was about to ask if everything was all right, but I changed it to "Isn't it awfully early for you to be up and about?"

"Yes, but neither one of us is packed yet, if you can believe it. There was just so much else to—but I wanted to call you and Dad and say thanks for all you did. I thought it went really well, didn't you?"

"It went perfectly," I said. "It was a *beautiful* wedding."

"Is Dad still with you?"

"Yes, we're just eating breakfast."

"Oh, sorry."

"No, no . . . Let me put him on," I said.

I held the receiver out to Max, and he stood up to take it. "Hey there," he said. And then, "Couldn't have gone better, I thought. What did Kenneth make of it?"

Darn, I should have asked that myself. I should have said something that showed that I'd moved on, that I'd forgotten there had ever been any issue with Kenneth.

"Good!" Max was saying. "He's exactly right. His folks supplied the glitz and then *your* folks dialed it down to a more reasonable level. Perfect teamwork."

I whispered, "Don't hang up when you're done."

"What?" Max asked me.

"I need to tell her one more thing."

"Okay," he said. "Deb? Hold on; your mom has something to add. So, have a good trip, hon. Bye." He handed me the receiver.

I said, "Sweetie, I just wanted to suggest that maybe you should call Sophie and Rupert and thank them too."

"I already did," Debbie said.

"Oh."

"They both agreed it was a big success, except Sophie thought the flowers weren't so great."

"What does *she* know?" I asked. And then, "Okay, sweetheart, I hope you have a wonderful honeymoon."

"Thanks, Mom."

I hung up. I told Max, "She phoned Sophie and Rupert before she phoned us."

"Well, sure," Max said. "They were the duty call. She wanted to get that over with."

"And she said Sophie thought the flowers weren't so great."

"And you said, 'What does *she* know?'" Max said. "As you should have."

We smiled at each other.

"So," Max said. "Do you still take a Sunday walk these days?"

"A . . . ? I don't necessarily have to," I said, because I didn't want to seem to be hustling him out the door. "I mean, it's not written in stone."

"I was just thinking I might come with you," he said.

"That would be very nice," I told him.

"Unless you'd prefer solitude."

"No, you're welcome to come along," I said.

Then I started eating my scrambled eggs. Before that, I'd been sort of dawdling.

My Sunday walk always followed a fixed course, passing the Ashton School at one point and including a fairly steep hill both coming and going, because I figured downhill worked a whole different set of leg muscles from uphill. The entire walk took exactly forty-five minutes. "Is forty-five minutes too long for you?" I asked Max.

"Not in the least," he said.

"Do you mind climbing a hill?"

"Who do you take me for?" he said. "I already told you, my doctor has me walking two miles daily."

"I just wanted to make sure."

He rolled his eyes. You couldn't blame me for asking, though. He was such a tub of a man, and he was wearing his usual crepe-soled shoes, whereas I always walked in Adidases the size of two watermelons.

I went upstairs to put them on as soon as we finished breakfast, and meanwhile Max cleaned up in the kitchen. It wasn't like him to be so conscientious. I started worrying that he felt sorry for me, first because I'd just said good-bye to my only daughter and then because I was about to be jobless. So when I came back downstairs, I made a point of acting brisk and unconcerned. "All set?" I asked. "You didn't bring any shorts, I don't suppose," because I myself had switched to clamdigger pants that hit just below my knees.

"No, all I have is these," he said, meaning the khakis that he'd arrived in.

"Well, luckily it's not so hot today."

Our exit from the house was complicated by the cat's suddenly taking it into her head to come with us. I was turning to shut the front door behind me when I felt something soft tickling my shins, and I said, "Whoa!" and nudged her back inside with the toe of one shoe. "What—is she accustomed to going outside?" I asked Max as I turned the key in the lock.

"I have no idea," he said.

"Because a lot of the neighbors have bird feeders," I told him, "and they would not be happy."

"I think it's more that she's gotten fond of you," he said. "She just wanted to come with you."

The man would not give up.

But I didn't bother debating the issue. "Right here is where we should cross," I told him, "because I see Fred Parrott pruning his hedge up ahead and he always has to stop everybody and talk and talk and talk. Then once we hit Tribal Lane, we'll hook a left and—"

"Or we could just wander any old which way," Max suggested.

I said, "I don't think so."

We passed the Nicholsons' house, and the place with the plaster Madonna in the yard. By then we were directly across from Fred Parrott. I said to Max, barely moving my lips, "Keep your head turned away or he'll flag us down."

We walked by with our faces averted.

"So, the people around here are friendly?" Max asked.

"More or less."

"Were any of them at the wedding?"

"At Debbie's wedding? No."

"How long have you been living here?"

"Twenty-one years," I said. "Twenty-one years in March."

Although he should know that as well as I did.

My father died in 2001, the fall of 2001. It wasn't unexpected—he'd had a lung condition for years—but when it finally happened, one Sunday afternoon as he was watching TV with my mother, I felt it came out of the blue. My mother took it much more in stride than I did. She dealt efficiently with the funeral arrangements and the paperwork, while I just basically sat there in a stunned heap. And it was she who informed me of the money he'd willed me, not a huge amount but a nice little chunk. I knew right away what I'd do with it. I don't even remember going through a decision process. I told Max before I went to bed that night that I wanted to buy someplace small where Debbie and I could live on our own. He himself, I said, could do whatever he chose—go on renting our current house, find himself an apartment, move to a whole other town, if he liked. It was entirely up to him.

"Are you saying . . . divorce?" Max asked me.

I said, "Right. Yes. I am."

"But *why*?" he said.

"Just because," I told him.

"Is it that guy?"

Even then, he didn't mention Andrew's name. Nor did I. "No," I said, "it's me."

"Great, Gail. The old 'It's not you, it's me' line."

"No," I told him. "This is more like 'It's not you; it's the me that I am when I'm with you.'"

"What?"

"I used to be . . ." I began.

I used to be the girl who stood in a vast golden field of wheat or oats or barley while Max Baines took my face between his palms as if it were something precious. He cupped my cheeks; he traced the scar on my chin with the tip of one thumb; he blinked as if he had trouble believing anyone could be so . . . well, perfect.

I used to be perfect.

But of course I couldn't say this aloud. What I said was, "I know I can't expect you to feel the same about me as you used to."

"What are you *talking* about?"

"Now, as for Debbie," I went on, "we're going to have to make this as stress-free for her as we can. We don't want her to feel torn between us. I'll let you see her whenever you like, of course; no quarrels about custody or anything like—"

"You'll *let* me see her?"

"I mean . . . you know what I mean," I said. "And she should never hear us arguing about it; she shouldn't see any sign of disagreement between us. We have to make it clear that we're on the same—"

"I *get* it," he said. Then he said, "You know what the operative word here is, Gail."

"The what?"

"The operative word is 'waste,'" he told me. "Sheer, pointless, empty *waste*."

And he walked out of the room.

This came as a relief, to be honest. It was high time he got angry! Let him go ahead and fume, let him clamp his lips and slam the door and pretend not to hear when I spoke to him. We could talk things over later, I thought.

We never did, though. Just a few days after that, he moved out. Rented an apartment down on St. Paul and packed all his belongings and vanished. No further discussion. That was harder than I had expected, I have to say. I had thought things would get simpler once we'd disentangled our two lives, but for a while they seemed more complicated. More subject to misunderstanding. I asked him on the phone once where he planned to take Debbie to supper and he said I had no right to cross-examine him. "I didn't meant to imply—" I said, but he'd already hung up. I invited him to her school play, and he said that of course he'd be there, because opening night happened to be one of her nights at his house; and that I should wait till the second performance before I came myself.

But after he took the job on the Eastern Shore, things got easier. The only times I saw him were when he came to Baltimore to pick Debbie up or drop her off, and gradually even those occasions grew less frequent, first because of the distance involved and then because Debbie developed a busy social life of her own as she grew older.

One time he phoned at the very last minute to cancel some

arrangement they'd made, and I said, "She'll be sorry to miss you," and he said, "She won't miss me."

"Of course she will!" I said, but he said, "Last week when I went to her school to pick her up she was out on the track field cheering."

"Cheering?"

"She was practicing one of those cheerleading chants that girls do at sports events. Jumping up in the air and waving these pompoms and then coming back down to earth and hugging the girl next to her and laughing her head off."

"Okay..." I said. Because of course she was laughing. She was fourteen years old at the time and she was with friends her own age. Only I knew how distressed she still was with both of us for what we had done to her life. (Go ahead, call me a coward; I never admitted to her that I alone was the one who had done it.)

But Max said, "She won't even notice I canceled."

"That's just not true," I told him.

But then only a month or so later, she came home from a weekend with him and said she was never going back. She said she didn't like his girlfriend. "His what?" I asked.

"She's fat," Debbie said.

"He has a girlfriend?"

"He has a girlfriend whose name is Roxanna and she's big as a house," Debbie said.

"Well... good for him," I said faintly.

Debbie made a snorting sound. "Grandma says men are just easily hoodwinked," she told me.

"Grandma! When did you talk to Grandma?"

"I, like, called her from Dad's place," she said.

"You . . . ?"

"I was upset, okay? And Grandma said men are just naturally weaker than women, so they can't admit they're getting old and that's why they leave their wives for young hussies."

"But that's not— Wait, Grandma said *hussies*?"

"Hussies who take advantage of married men in their moment of weakness."

"Debbie, please do not use the word 'hussies.'"

"I didn't use it! Grandma did."

"I can't believe that," I said.

"You think I'm lying?"

"No, I—but your grandma hasn't the slightest notion what she's talking about, trust me."

"Anyhow," Debbie said. "You don't have to worry about *me*. I already know I'm going to be a nun."

"Oh, stop; you're not even Catholic," I said.

"So will you call Dad and tell him I'm not ever coming back?"

"You call him," I said. "I'm staying out of it."

Because I do know how to do *some* things right.

Although I admit that I had a few bad weeks there, after I heard about Roxanna. I had to give myself a stern talking-to. ("Face up, Gail," I said. "This is exactly what you deserve," I said.)

As for Debbie, maybe she called Max and maybe she didn't; I never inquired. And after a brief interval, she did resume her visits to him. For one thing, in January of the following year she got her driver's license, which meant she could borrow my car—a huge inducement, at least during that early stage when driving is a novelty. She never lost her dismissive tone when she referred to Roxanna, but eventually I noticed, tucked in her bedroom mirror frame, a snapshot of her and a woman who had to be Roxanna standing in some kind of farmer's market, and they had their arms slung around each other and Debbie was smiling and relaxed looking. What's more, Roxanna was beautiful. Till then I'd felt sort of smug about her much-vaunted obesity, but some overweight women are so lush and creamy-skinned and sublimely confident that you have to wonder why thinness is considered an asset. There were dimples in both her cheeks, and she had lovely, pillowy mounds of breasts and a gentle curve of a belly.

I can't recall when it was that Debbie stopped mentioning her. It just dawned on me, after a couple of years or so, that Roxanna's photo was no longer in Debbie's mirror frame. And something Max said later, when a divorced friend of ours remarried ("Getting married would be so much work, after a certain age," he said), made me wonder if he and Roxanna were simply at two different stages in their lives.

At any rate: time passed, and whatever dealings Max and I had became more matter-of-fact. He and I attended Debbie's high school graduation together, and then her college graduation. We sat side by side for the awarding of her law degree, and on a couple of occasions he and Debbie came to my house for dinner when he happened to be spending the night with her.

A while back, when the nurse at my school was going through a divorce, she told me, "What I'm aiming for is that Steve and I should have a civilized friendship with each other, the way you and *your* ex do."

"We do?" I said. And then, "Oh. We do."

I didn't tell her how many years of ups and downs and icy silences and hurt feelings we'd had to go through to get there.

The sun felt a lot warmer now. The rows of houses became rows of shops intermingled with smaller houses, and then the houses turned into podiatry offices or one-man insurance agencies, and then we took a right onto Ashton Street and I saw Mayella's Produce and the lake trout joint and beyond that, my school. Which reminded me: "I was thinking," I said (a bit breathlessly, on account of the hill we'd just climbed), "maybe I should send Marilee an email wishing her well with her procedure."

"What procedure is that?" Max asked.

"She's having a cardio-something tomorrow to change the rate of her heartbeat."

"That sounds serious," Max said.

"Cardio...gram? Graph? Cardiolysis? I didn't have a chance to wish her well on Friday because she was so busy questioning my people skills, but I can see where I might have sounded a bit, maybe, uncaring."

"If you want to prove your people skills you should telephone her, not email."

"Oh, that would be false advertising," I said, only half joking. "I don't have *that* many people skills. Besides, what's wrong with emailing? We might even say it shows respect. Respecting her private time with her husband the day before her... cardioxy?"

"Phone calls convey a more immediate concern," Max said. "Like, 'Forgive me for intruding, but I've been sitting here feeling so worried about you that I just had to pick up the phone and ask you what I can do.'"

I said, "Ha! She would wonder what had gotten into me."

The Ashton School was closed and silent, I saw, with all the classroom shades pulled down to exactly the same level just as our custodian liked them; no bothersome teachers or students interfering with his preferences. Once we'd walked past it, we made a U-turn and started back the way we had come. I said, "I hate forgetting words. Hunting through my memory for them; it's like asking the Magic 8 Ball, you know? 'Will I be rich when I'm grown?' 'Will I travel?' And then waiting for the answer to float up slowly, slowly in the glass."

"'It is not yet clear,'" Max intoned in a solemn voice. "'Ask again later.'"

"But at least it *did* float up, when I was young. Now that I'm old, it sometimes doesn't. I'll say, 'It will come to me by and by,' but it doesn't."

"Yeah, welcome to the club," Max said lightly.

"I hate it," I told him.

He looked over at me.

I said, "It makes me feel . . . vulnerable."

"Oh," he said. "Sweetheart."

"But you're right: welcome to the club!" I said. "Gosh, is that a red-winged blackbird?" And we both turned to watch it fly up from a mulberry bush, black as ink with its epaulettes of startling scarlet.

"You and I were going to grow old side by side, once upon a time," Max said.

I don't know where he expected *that* remark to go. I didn't answer, and we walked the rest of the way in silence.

Even though I hadn't let on at the time, I thought seriously about his advice to wish Marilee well by phone. He might have a point, I thought. So after we came home, while I was upstairs changing out of my walking clothes, I sat down on the edge of my bed to give her a call. I had to look up her number in my little bedside phonebook; that's how seldom I phoned her.

"Gail!" she said when she picked up.

"Hi, Marilee."

"I'm glad you got back to me."

"Right," I said. I'd forgotten all about her answering machine message. "Well, I just wanted to say I'm hoping things will go well tomorrow."

"Why, thank you," she said. "That's very thoughtful of you. Now. What I'd called about. Please don't take this the wrong way, but I happened to remember that before you hired on as my assistant, you were teaching math at Millwood High."

"Yes..."

"Teaching remedial math."

"Right."

"So on Friday after you left I phoned Emmy Lawton," she said.

Emmy was head of the mathematics department at our school—not terribly bright, but I liked her.

"I asked if she had any interest in acquiring a specialist in remedial math," she said, "and she said absolutely she did. Ever since Covid times set our students so far back, she said... But, so, I don't want you to feel insulted by this suggestion; I realize you've long since moved up in the world..."

Count on Marilee to imagine that administration was a move up in the world.

"Still, would you ever consider the possibility of going back to teaching?" she asked.

"You mean at the Ashton School," I said.

"At least mull it over?"

"Huh. It's a thought," I told her. And it was—but kind of a complicated thought. I set it aside, for the time being. I said, "So, maybe your husband could give me a call tomorrow to tell me how things went with you."

"Thank you. I'll let him know," she said.

It would have sounded more personal if I'd remembered her husband's first name. I didn't, though.

After I'd hung up I crossed the hall to the guest room, where Max was packing. "I did it," I told him.

"Did what?" he asked.

"I phoned Marilee to wish her well."

"Excellent," he said.

"And she happened to mention that the Ashton School could use a remedial math teacher."

"Oh," he said. "I see."

To myself I said, "Darn. I should have asked *her* what that cardio procedure's called."

"Now, promise you won't get mad at this," Max said.

I looked over at him. I braced myself.

"But I did just now phone Sam Levy," he said. "I asked if by any chance we needed a remedial math teacher at *our* school. And he said, 'Are you kidding? I would kill for a remedial math teacher.'"

"Who would he kill?" I asked.

"Whom," Max said. And then, "Are you mad?"

"No," I said. "You were nice to go to the trouble."

"It's only that I was thinking change is sometimes a good thing, don't you find?"

"Right," I said. "Except, *you* know. Here I am in Baltimore."

"Yes," he said. "I know."

"Hey!" I said. "I have an idea. Are you leaving right away? Because if you don't mind sticking around awhile, I could invite you out to lunch before you go."

"I'd be happy to stick around."

"Lunch at the Cultured Crab, maybe, since you get such a kick out of the place. How does that sound?"

"That would be very nice," he said.

After that I ran out of things to say, so I went on downstairs.

I was reading the Sunday *Sun* on the couch next to the cat when Max came down himself. "Care for some of the paper?" I asked him, and he said, "Thanks," and accepted the front section and took it over to the rocker. "Do I really want to know this?" he asked the top headline as he sat down.

I went back to reading the "Ask Amy" column. I'd always liked how Amy doesn't put up with any nonsense. "Darn right!" I said aloud at one point. "The *nerve* of some people!" and the cat sent me an uneasy glance and edged a few inches away.

"The pay would not be that great, I grant you," Max said. He seemed to be speaking again to the newspaper headlines. "But you should bear in mind that the cost of living is much lower there."

"You mean . . . on the Eastern Shore?" I asked him.

He looked over at me, finally. "You could pick up a really nice house for practically nothing," he told me.

"Well, sure; it's a depressed area," I said.

He said, "As if Baltimore isn't depressed!" And then, "Just think, though: once Debbie and Kenneth have kids they can bring them for summer vacations. I suggest you bear that in mind when you're considering how many rooms you'll need."

"You're talking as if it would be a beach house," I said, "but the cost of living at the beach is astronomical."

"No, I'm talking about *my* neck of the woods," he said, "Cornboro. They could stay with you in Cornboro and then drive to the nearest beach every day in not much more than an hour."

"Oh, you're right," I said. "And the drive would be so undemanding that Kenny Junior can take the wheel as soon as he gets his learner's permit."

Max looked confused, but only for a second. "True enough," he agreed.

"Max," I said. "I appreciate the thought. But the fact is that I believe I have only one span of life allotted to me. I don't feel I have the option of just . . . trying out various random ideas and giving up if they don't work out."

"Yes, well," Max said with a sigh.

He himself, apparently, assumed he had an infinite number of lives.

Someday I'd like to be given credit for all the times I have *not* said something that I could have said.

⁂

For our lunch outing we took my car, since I needed to gas up before heading to work on Monday. (I was beginning to acknowledge that I might not be quitting quite yet.) The car's interior still smelled faintly of hair product, I noticed. I rolled down my window before we took off. "Let's do the gas on the way back," I told Max. "I'm starving, all at once."

"Me too," he said.

The Cultured Crab was in Lutherville, near where he had grown up. It had been his parents' chosen restaurant for important family occasions. Now that they were long gone you would think it would make him sad to go back, but it didn't seem to. He gazed out his window contentedly as we traveled up the York Road corridor, with its mishmash of car dealers and barbecue joints and strip malls and discount tire warehouses. "When Deb told me she and Kenneth were getting married," he said, "I took the two of them to the Cultured Crab for a celebration dinner. Did she happen to mention that?"

"No. What did Kenneth think of it?"

"He loved it."

"Although, what else was he going to say?"

"No, seriously, I think he really did. He said it was one of a kind."

"Well, *that* I can believe," I said.

"But I should warn you," Max said. "Since Covid times, the place has undergone a bit of a conversion."

"Oh!" I said suddenly. "Cardio*version!*"

"What?"

"Marilee's procedure. It's called a cardioversion."

"Ah."

"This jolt to her heart to make it start beating right."

"Modern medicine," he marveled. "Okay, so, what they did was set up a lot of outdoor tables à la French sidewalk café, and they still haven't taken them away. You see what I'm talking about."

Because by now we were nearing the restaurant. The façade was unchanged—a white clapboard cube with a neon crab in a chef's toque dancing on the roof—but the space out front had become a jumble of tables and chairs and collapsed umbrellas, all bordered by the trash bins and newspaper boxes lined up as usual along the edge of the curb. "Paris, France," he said with a wave.

"I see," I said.

"Just don't tell them you're too fool."

"Right."

That's something you forget when you've been on your own awhile: those married-couple conversations that continue intermittently for weeks, sometimes, branching out and doubling back and looping into earlier strands like a piece of crochet work.

I found a parking space a short distance up ahead, and we got out of the car and threaded our way between the outdoor tables. None of them were occupied, and when we stepped inside the café we found most of those tables empty as well. A young woman seated near the window was nursing a cocktail, while two older men across the room studied their menus with their foreheads knotted in frowns. I was fairly sure I know *why* they were frowning. They had probably wandered in assuming this was your average Baltimore seafood joint. The idea behind the Cultured Crab, though, was that it was more upscale. Ordinary steamed crabs weren't even on the menu—too messy, too much work for the diners. The crabcakes, so-called, were thumb-size croquettes studded with charred shishito pepper bits. Crab parfait layered with wasabi-spiked crème fraîche. Crab salad with marcona almonds under a yuzu glaze. Max's parents had taken this food seriously, but Max himself found it hilarious. As we walked in he was actually rubbing his hands together, and the minute we had been seated by the hostess (a thirteen-year-old, from the looks of her), he had to read the tablecloth. Each tablecloth was different—an Irish linen facsimile of a newspaper page, meant to duplicate the actual newspapers where other crabhouses dumped their vats of steamed whole crabs. Our particular page included reports of a city council oyster roast and a squeegee-kid party where the mayor himself had handed out hot crab heroes. That one Max read aloud. I said, "Notice they don't say *which* mayor."

"It's like a time warp," Max said. He was gazing now at a corner table across the room. "Remember when we were all sitting over there and my sister announced she was pregnant?"

"Oh, Lord," I said, because his sister had not been married back then.

"And Dad stood up so suddenly that he knocked against the table edge and our candlestick fell over and set Mom's menu on fire."

"Happy days," I said.

"Would you guys care to start with a drink?" our waitress asked us. She seemed to be another teenager. Evidently all the "hon"-type waitresses in their sixties had taken early retirement during the pandemic. "Just water, please," I told her, and Max said, "I'll have the iced tea." The Cultured Crab's iced tea was famous; it was seasoned with cumin or turmeric or some such that turned people's teeth yellow.

"And now that baby is a grown woman who just attended our daughter's wedding," Max said once we were alone again. Evidently he was back on the subject of his sister's pregnancy.

"She's getting a few gray hairs, even," I said. "I noticed while we were talking together after the ceremony."

I was scanning my menu as I spoke, trying to find the least bizarre combination. I've never been a fan of foods I didn't eat in my childhood. The tin-can taste of mango, the bad-breath taste of cilantro—I might have been fine with them if I'd met them as a three-year-old. Max, of course, went in the opposite direction. Now he said, "What do you guess asafoetida is?"

"I hate to even imagine," I said. Then I said, "You know what 'cardioversion' makes me think of?"

"What," he said.

"Remember in the old days, when people used to tap their watches?"

"They still do, if they're smartwatches," he told me.

"Those are not *watches*; they're computers on wristbands. But a normal watch like mine," I said, "why would I need to tap it, these days? It runs for years on one battery."

"Why would you tap it even back then?" he asked me. "Though come to think of it," he added, "my grandfather used to tap his watch when he wanted to point out how late we were."

"Yes, so did my dad," I said. "But I guess it could also mean the opposite. Like, 'Is this thing *dead*? Because I could swear I've been at this party for hours, but my watch says it's only eight thirty.'"

"Or also, 'Stop right here, watch. Stop exactly where you are now.'"

"Well, I've never seen *that* one," I said. "And let's hope not in Marilee's case. We're talking about a heart, remember."

"Or 'Go backward, watch,'" Max said.

"Backward!"

Our waitress set down our glasses and asked, "Have you guys decided yet?"

"I'll have the crab and-rhubarb strata," Max told her.

"If that's your decision," she said.

I said, "I'll have the rockfish, minus the honey-sumac sauce."

"You got it."

She took our menus from us and left. No sign of pen and paper, but I guess at her age she felt she could trust her memory.

Max said, "Haven't these past three days felt like going backward in time together?"

"Like *Groundhog Day*," I agreed.

"Groundhog Day?" He looked puzzled. "Scared of our shadows?"

"*Groundhog Day* the movie," I told him. Count on Max; he wasn't much of a moviegoer. "Where people live through the same one day over and over until they get it right."

"Exactly," Max said. "We've been given another chance to get it right."

"And yet, did we?" I asked. "You show up uninvited, just the same as when you moved in with me and my roommates after Polly got married. You bring an unannounced pet, just the same as when you brought your dog."

"It's true," Max said happily. "And, hey! We even had Jared Johnson hanging around again!"

"Yes, come to think of it."

"We even had your losing-your-job issue."

"Right."

"So, how many times did it take them?" he asked.

"Take whom?"

"The people in *Groundhog Day*. How many times till they got it right?"

"Lots," I said. "I lost count, in fact."

"Wouldn't that be great?" he asked me. "If the world really worked that way?"

I'd been about to say that it had taken them so many times that I had very nearly walked out of the movie in the middle, but instead I said, "Well, yes, it would, I guess."

Then our waitress came back to tell us, "I forgot to mention our special appetizer: raw shrimp in tequila with salmon roe."

"No!" we said—even Max—and she went away again.

After lunch, we stopped to buy gas at the nearest Exxon station. "I'll do this," Max announced as we pulled in, but I said, "No, no, I will," because I worried he would insist on paying for it. (We'd already argued about my paying for our meal, even though I was the one who'd invited him.) I hopped out of the car before he could and unhooked the pump nozzle, which meant I accidentally skipped the step where I should have pressed my gas tank's release tab. So Max got to act all patient and forbearing as he leaned across from his seat and pressed it himself. "I was *going* to do that!" I told him. "I've done it a million times."

Long story short, therefore: I ended up with hands that smelled like gasoline. So when we got back to my house, the cat took one whiff of me at the front door and then promptly vanished, straight up the stairs. "Celine?" I called after her.

Max said, "Who?"

I said, "Oh, the . . . cat." I turned away. I went to hang my purse in the closet. "Honestly!" I said. "Such a delicate flower, she is."

"Wait, her name is Celine?" he asked.

"No, silly. I just had to call her something in a pinch," I said. I closed the closet door.

"So, does this mean you might want to keep her?" he asked, trailing after me into the living room.

"No, no. It just means I don't believe in letting an animal walk around nameless," I told him.

"Oh."

He stuffed his hands in his pockets. "Okay," he said. "Well, I guess I ought to go finish packing."

"You're leaving right now?" I asked him.

"I thought I would."

"I figured you'd want your nap first."

"No, I should get out of your hair," he said.

I said, "All right." And then, "Although it's not as if I have anything else to do today. You're welcome to take your nap if you like."

"No, that's okay," he said, and he turned and started up the stairs.

I would have called the cat again, but I felt self-conscious about repeating her name in Max's hearing. Instead I went out to the kitchen and checked my answering machine. One message: my mother. "Hello, dear," the recording said. "Sorry I missed you! I hope you're not feeling too bereft after the wedding."

Bereft was exactly how I was feeling. But I wasn't sure I could blame the wedding. I stood looking at the phone, knowing I should call her back and yet putting it off. And then the cat wandered in of her own accord. "Hey there," I told her. She brushed against my ankles invitingly, but before I picked her up I went over to the sink and thoroughly washed my hands and forearms, all the way to my elbows. Then I dried off and gave one wrist a sniff. Not too bad, in my opinion. And when I stooped to gather her up, she didn't try to escape. She herself smelled like clean woolens. I buried my nose in her neck and drew in a deep breath of her, and then I carried her out of the kitchen and up the stairs. At the guest room doorway, I paused to watch Max folding a shirt. He kept his eyes on what he was doing, though, as if he were still alone.

"So, I'm wondering," I told him. "Suppose I *did* decide to keep the cat; didn't you say your shelter would object if you didn't bring her back with you?"

Now he looked up. He stopped folding his shirt. "You mean, keep her for good?" he asked.

"Because she does seem comfortable here," I said.

"Oh, she loves it here! She loves it! You won't regret this, Gail, I promise. As for the shelter: you'd just need to fill out some paperwork, but I can email you that. It might be a bit more complicated because you live in a different state, is all."

"That's okay," I said.

I hoped I wasn't going to regret this.

"Now, about her supplies," he said. "Her litter box and such. Her bag of kibble. Why don't I just leave you with what I brought. We're allowed to, when the new owner's not equipped yet."

"Thank you," I said.

"This is great!" he told me.

"Right," I said.

I stood there a moment longer. He laid the shirt in the duffel bag on his bed and went over to the closet.

"So . . . that's all settled, I guess," I said finally, and I turned to carry the cat back downstairs.

When I reached the living room, she jumped out of my arms like someone who'd just accomplished something. She proceeded straight to the kitchen, and I followed to watch her start picking at her bowl of kibble.

I would need to buy a dedicated feeding dish, I decided. In fact, maybe a continuous feeder, for when I was out of the house. And cat treats. The whole time she had been here, I'd been wishing I had some cat treats to entice her with.

Would she like a scratching post? What cat *wouldn't* like a scratching post? Maybe one of those tree-shaped affairs with several levels to it. I could set it by a window so she could watch birds to her heart's content.

I heard Max's footsteps upstairs, but they weren't drawing any closer. Finally I settled on the couch, and the cat wandered in a moment later and sat on the rug to wash her face. Now Max finally did cross the hall and start down the stairs. I stayed seated, though.

"All set," he said as he arrived in the living room. He had his duffel bag slung over one shoulder and he was clutching the Lerner Brothers bag. "So, the cat has been chipped," he told me, "and all her shots are up to date."

"Chipped?" I asked.

"Electronically, by the vet. In case you ever need to verify her records. Also, I don't foresee any complications with the out-of-state issue, but I'll check into all that before I send you the paperwork."

"Thank you," I said.

"No, thank *you*!" he said. Then he said, "It's another *Groundhog* moment, right? You didn't want my dog at first, either, but then you got into a knock-down-drag-out fight with your roommates to keep them from evicting her."

He was exaggerating, of course. I'd just had a civilized discussion with them. But I said, "Well, sure, because that was Barbara! Good old Barb."

"Good old Barb," he agreed. Then he turned to the cat and said, "So long, Miss Celine. You've found yourself a pretty cushy berth, let me assure you."

Celine went on washing her face industriously.

"She's pretending not to hear," he told me, "in case I still have any plans to take her with me."

Then he headed toward the front door, and I rose to follow him. The day was downright hot now, I could tell the instant I stepped outside. I said, "It's lucky we took our walk early."

"Yup."

We descended the front steps. I said, "I didn't think to ask whether you're working this summer."

"Only part-time," he said. "Some of our kids do stay on if they don't have anyplace else to go, but in summer it's more like a day camp."

"That sounds nice," I said.

"Yup."

We stopped beside his car. It was a decent distance from my own car, for once, since I'd been the last to park. He unlocked his trunk to put his duffel bag inside, and then he chucked the Lerner Brothers bag in after it.

I said, "What's the name of your school, again? I forget."

"Cornboro Special," he said.

"Ah, yes."

An unfortunate choice, I'd aways thought. "Special" sounded faintly suspect. But of course I didn't say so. I just stood smiling and looking into his face. He didn't pursue the subject, though. He said, "Okay, then, I guess. Thanks for letting me stay with you."

"Anytime," I told him.

He lifted one palm in a sort of salute, and then he went around to the driver's side and got in and started the engine. I watched until his car turned left at the end of the block before I went back to the house.

Celine hadn't stirred from the rug, but she'd progressed from face-washing to shin-washing. "Hi, sweetheart," I told her. She didn't look up. I went to the kitchen and loaded a couple of glasses into the dishwasher. Wiped off a counter. Hung up a towel. Pulled a chair out from the table and sat down to phone my mother, finally.

"Hi, Mom," I said when she answered. "Sorry it took me a while to get back to you. I still had Max here till a minute ago."

"Well, I just called to make sure you're not missing your girl," she said.

"No, I'm okay. I mean, of course I miss her, but I'm happy the wedding went well. She did phone earlier today to say she'd enjoyed it."

"Yes, she phoned me too," Mom said.

"Oh, good. And I know she called Sophie and Rupert."

In fact, should I be concerned that she'd spent so much time with us all on the phone instead of focusing on her new husband?

No, I thought. Let that go.

"It must have been quite a strain having Max around for this long," Mom was saying.

"Not at all," I said. "We even went out to lunch today before he left. At the Cultured Crab."

"Ooh! Do tell," Mom said, "what'd you order?"

"Just, I don't know. A fish thing. And I'm keeping that cat he brought."

"You're not," Mom said.

"She's turned out to be really nice."

"But what will you do when Kenneth comes over?"

"Kenneth," I said. "Well, I don't think it's *that* big a problem. He can just use his . . . whatchamacallit if he gets wheezy."

"Have it your way," she said. "You know I'm not a huge cat fan. I've always felt they were coldhearted."

"Cats are not coldhearted!" I said. "They're only protecting their dignity, in case they get rejected. 'I'll just reject you first,' they're saying."

"Yes, so you've always told me."

"Anyhow," I said. "I'll be in touch later this week, okay? Maybe we can go to a movie together, if there's anything worth seeing."

"That would be lovely," she said. "Good-bye, dear."

"Bye, Mom."

I hung up.

I went back to the living room. I sank down on the couch. It was more like collapsing, really.

What was I supposed to do with the rest of my life?

I'm too young for this, I thought. Not too old, as you might expect, but too young, too inept, too uninformed. How come there weren't any *grownups* around? Why did everyone just assume I knew what I was doing?

It was a good thing I had Celine. She had hopped up beside me by now, and I could busy myself with running the tip of an index finger along the length of her elegant nose, which made her close her eyes and purr.

What I should have told Max was . . .

What I should have asked . . .

What I should have made clear to him . . .

Oh, why was I so *bottled up?*

How was it that, standing in a field of gold, I had not had the faintest idea whether it was wheat or rye or barley? Why had I registered Max's awe as he cupped my face, his look of utter adoration, but given not one passing thought to whether *I* had adored *him?*

The doorbell rang, but I ignored it. The cat, however, fled instantaneously, without even seeming to collect herself for her leap.

Until now, I had imagined that I'd been drawn to Andrew Mason because he was so unknowable. In fact, though, I had known him all too well. I *was* him. I had recognized his separateness, and his held-back smile, and his absolute certainty that since he took his own coffee black, there was no need whatsoever to set out cream and sugar for anybody else.

From the front porch, I heard a man call, "Gail?"

I told myself that this was . . . I don't know. A neighbor? Someone from school? The only reason it sounded like Max was that I'd just been thinking of Max.

I rose and went to open the door. "I had this sudden idea," Max told me. He was standing back a bit with his hands down at his sides, as if to prove that he meant no harm. "This idea about the adoption papers. You know what might be easiest? If we put *my* name on the papers. I'm a Delaware resident."

I said, "Oh." I said, "I hadn't considered that."

"With your name too, though, I'm saying. Yours and mine both, jointly. It wouldn't be a lie, exactly. Especially not if you came to live in Cornboro, by and by."

Then he tilted his head. "Gail?" he asked. "Do you think?"

The year was 2023, and nearly every man, woman, and child in America owned a cell phone, including Max Baines. He could have called me while he was driving. Or pulled over to the side of the road and called. Or even waited till he got home and called me then. And yet here he was in person, standing on my front porch.

Which gave me the courage, finally, to step out onto the porch myself and cup his face in my hands. I studied his sweet, bristly cheeks, and the satiny skin below his brown eyes, and his forehead creased with concern, and I committed them all to memory before I kissed him.

End

A NOTE ABOUT THE AUTHOR

Anne Tyler was born in Minneapolis, Minnesota, in 1941 and grew up in Raleigh, North Carolina. She graduated at nineteen from Duke University and went on to do graduate work in Russian studies at Columbia University. She is the author of more than twenty novels. Her twentieth novel, *A Spool of Blue Thread*, was short-listed for the Man Booker Prize in 2015. Her eleventh novel, *Breathing Lessons*, was awarded the Pulitzer Prize in 1988. She is a member of the American Academy of Arts and Letters. She lives in Baltimore, Maryland.

A NOTE ON THE TYPE

This book was set in a typeface called Walbaum. The original cutting of this face was made by Justus Erich Walbaum (1768–1839) in Weimar in 1810. The type was revived by the Monotype Corporation in 1934. Young Walbaum began his artistic career as an apprentice to a maker of cookie molds. How he managed to leave this field and become a successful punch cutter remains a mystery. Although the type that bears his name may be classified as modern, numerous slight irregularities in its cut give this face its humane manner.

*Composed by North Market Street Graphics,
Lancaster, Pennsylvania*

*Printed and bound by Berryville Graphics,
Berryville, Virginia*

Designed by Casey Hampton